PRAISE FOR *DEATH OF A LIAR*
and M. C. BEATON'S ACCLAIMED MYSTERIES
FEATURING HAMISH MACBETH

"Longing for escape? Tired of waiting for Brigadoon to materialize? Time for a trip to Lochdubh, the scenic, if somnolent, village in the Scottish Highlands where M. C. Beaton sets her beguiling whodunits featuring Constable Hamish Macbeth." —*New York Times Book Review*

"Hamish Macbeth is that most unusual character, one to whom the reader returns because of his charming flaws. May he never get promoted."

—*New York Journal of Books*

"With residents and a constable so authentic, it won't be long before tourists will be seeking Lochdubh and believing in the reality of Hamish Macbeth as surely as they believed in Sherlock Holmes."

—*Denver Rocky Mountain News*

"Macbeth is the sort of character who slyly grows on you." —*Chicago Sun-Times*

"On a scale of one to ten, M. C. Beaton's Constable Hamish Macbeth merits a ten plus." —*Buffalo News*

"The thirtieth mystery in the Hamish Macbeth series is exceptionally entertaining and fast paced…What makes her Macbeth series stand out is the deft depiction of a

Highlands village, with all its beauties and tensions and, especially, the complicated, endearing character of Macbeth himself, who wants nothing more than to lead a quiet life enjoying the beauty that surrounds him, if only women wouldn't keep getting in his way."

—*Booklist* (starred review)

"Beaton has surpassed herself with the Lochdubh residents."

—*Woman's Way*

"This Hamish Macbeth mystery is as quirky as the others. Hamish is an endearing character who coincidentally happens upon all sorts of mischief and finds himself wrapped up in the center of a murder investigation that hits close to home."

—*RT Reviews*

"Highly entertaining…Beaton's series remains as engaging as ever."

—*Publishers Weekly*

Death *of a* Liar

More Hamish Macbeth Mysteries by M. C. Beaton

Death of a Nurse
Death of a Liar
Death of a Policeman
Death of Yesterday
Death of a Kingfisher
Death of a Chimney Sweep
Death of a Valentine
Death of a Witch
Death of a Gentle Lady
Death of a Maid
Death of a Dreamer
Death of a Bore
Death of a Poison Pen
Death of a Village
Death of a Celebrity
Death of a Dustman
Death of an Addict
Death of a Scriptwriter
Death of a Dentist
Death of a Macho Man
Death of a Nag
Death of a Charming Man
Death of a Travelling Man
Death of a Greedy Woman
Death of a Prankster
Death of a Snob
Death of a Hussy
Death of a Perfect Wife
Death of an Outsider
Death of a Cad
Death of a Gossip
A Highland Christmas

M. C. BEATON

Death *of a* Liar

GRAND CENTRAL
PUBLISHING

NEW YORK   BOSTON

Copyright © 2015 by Marion Chesney

Preview of *Death of a Nurse* copyright © 2016 by Marion Chesney

Grand Central Publishing
Hachette Book Group
1290 Avenue of the Americas
New York, NY 10104
www.HachetteBookGroup.com

Grand Central Publishing is a division of Hachette Book Group, Inc. The Grand Central Publishing name and logo are trademarks of Hachette Book Group, Inc.

The Hachette Speakers Bureau provides a wide range of authors for speaking events. To find out more, go to www.hachettespeakersbureau.com or call (866) 376-6591.

The publisher is not responsible for websites (or their content) that are not owned by the publisher.

Printed in the United States of America

Originally published in hardcover by Hachette Book Group
First mass market edition: January 2016

10 9 8 7 6 5 4 3 2 1
OPM

This book is dedicated to my friend Cheryl Price; her father, Malcolm; mother, Jenny; brother, Rupert; nephew, Jack; and boyfriend, Ben Sawbridge.

Death *of a* Liar

Chapter One

☠

Then one day there really was a wolf, but when the boy shouted they didn't believe him.

—Aesop

Police Sergeant Hamish Macbeth and his sidekick, Dick Fraser, sat in deck chairs in the front garden of the police station enjoying the Indian summer and the fact that the county of Sutherland in the very north of Scotland seemed free of crime.

At Hamish's feet lay his wild cat, Sonsie, and his dog, Lugs, as lazy as their master. The berries on the rowan tree at the gate gleamed as red as Hamish's hair.

The air had that clear, sparkling quality as there was no pollution. The sky was blue, the sun shone down, and Dick folded his chubby hands across his plump stomach and fell asleep.

The sudden shrilling of the phone inside the police station cut through the air. Hamish went in to answer it, not expecting anything important, for what nasty thing could happen on such a lovely day?

At first he could not make out what the woman on the line was saying.

"Calm down," said Hamish in his soft highland accent. "Take a deep breath. Now, what's happened?"

"It's me, Liz Bentley, at Cromish. I've been raped. Oh, help me!"

"I'll be with you as fast as I can," said Hamish.

He went into the garden and roused Dick. "Some woman up at Cromish says she's been raped. Let's go."

Soon Hamish, Dick, and the animals were all in the police Land Rover and heading out of Lochdubh and up the west coast of Sutherland to Cromish.

It was a long drive, the village of Cromish being situated between Kinlochbervie and Cape Wrath. Sutherland, the south land of the Vikings, covers three hundred thirty-five square kilometres but has a population of only thirteen thousand people, making it one of the most sparsely populated areas in the United Kingdom.

There are villages like Cromish which look as if time had forgotten them. The fishing boom had come and gone, leaving only a small huddled group of cottages beside a crumbling harbour. The mountains of Foinaven, Arkle, and Ben Stack loomed in the distance. Like Lochdubh, it boasted only one shop, a post office, and a general store, run, as Hamish remembered, by an old woman.

They quickly found Liz Bentley's address. She was a short woman with rosy cheeks and brown hair. When she saw Hamish, she threw herself into his arms and began to cry.

"There, there, lassie," said Hamish, although Liz was somewhere, he guessed, in her fifties. "Let's go ben and tell me about it. Make us some tea, Dick."

He settled her down in an armchair and waited until she had dried her eyes. "Now, first, have you called the doctor?"

"No, why?"

"You'll need to be examined and then you'll have to go to hospital where they'll take a swab for DNA."

"It won't do any good," she said. "I was that shamed and disgusted, I burnt my clothes and took a swim in the sea."

"Nonetheless, you'll need to be examined for signs of rape. What is the local doctor's name?"

"Dr. Williams."

"Number?"

"It's on the wall by the phone, but he's awfy busy and…"

Hamish ignored her, phoned the doctor, and explained it was an emergency. The doctor said he would be there right away.

"So," said Hamish, returning to her. "Tell me what happened. What did he look like?"

"I couldnae see his face. He had a black balaclava

on. He was awfy tall and strong. He threw me to the floor and held a knife to my throat."

"And when did this happen?"

"Last night. About midnight. I hadn't locked the door."

"Why didn't you report it sooner?"

"He said if I called the police, he would murder me!"

Dick came in with a mug of tea which he handed to Liz. The doorbell rang. "That'll be the doctor," said Hamish.

Dr. Williams was a small, gnarled man with a sagging grey face. "Let's go into the bedroom, Liz," he said.

"I'm not up to it!" wailed Liz.

"Now, then, I haven't got a case if you won't help me," said Hamish. "Off you go."

As Liz was reluctantly led off to the bedroom, Hamish looked around the room. It showed all the signs of that old-fashioned practice of "being kept for best."

The fireplace was empty. Above it hung a gilt-framed mirror. The sofa was an antique one, stuffed with horsehair but looking as new as it had probably done a hundred years before. A table by the window was covered with an embroidered cloth and had a shiny aspidistra in a brass bowl. There were two armchairs, covered in chintz. On an occasional table, a pink china lady held up a pink frilled lamp shade.

Hamish strolled outside and let the dog and cat out

of the Land Rover. He would wait for the doctor's report and then question the villagers to see if they had noticed any stranger in the area.

"Officer!"

Hamish swung round. Dr. Williams came up to him.

"I'm afraid you have had a wasted journey."

"What makes you say that?"

"Because Liz Bentley is a virgin, that's what. Furthermore, she's a chronic liar. Last year, she told everyone she had terminal cancer when I was away on holiday. The villagers were so sympathetic they gave her little gifts. I soon discovered when I came back that it was all lies. She said she was attending the hospital at Strathbane for chemotherapy. I phoned them up and they'd never heard of her. When I challenged her, she said it was a miracle. She had prayed and prayed and God had taken the cancer away."

"I'll chust be having a wee word with her," said Hamish, the sudden sibilance of his accent showing he was really angry.

He strode into the parlour where Liz was sobbing on Dick's bosom.

"She's a damn liar," said Hamish. "Leave her alone. Stop the waterworks, Liz, and hear this. I should charge you with wasting police time and get you to pay for the petrol it cost to get here. I suggest you start to see a psychiatrist. Don't effer dare phone me again. Come on, Dick."

*   *   *

"It's called Munchausen syndrome," said Dick as they drove off. "You know, it's where a body keeps lying to get attention. I mind a case in Strathbane where a woman kept making her children sick so that everyone would sympathise with her."

"Pah!" said Hamish. "Let's find somewhere to eat."

They stopped at the Kinlochbervie Hotel and had a pleasant lunch in the bistro.

"It's a sad thing to have a mental problem like that," said Dick. "I mean, they cannae stop."

"Do you mean that damn woman is going to plague us with another lie?" said Hamish.

"She'll probably make herself ill or something."

But Lochdubh, during the next week, settled down into its peaceful ways. The only great change in the village was that the old schoolhouse had been closed down and the children were now bussed into Strathbane. The school had been turned into a house and had just been bought by an English couple, a Mr. and Mrs. Leigh.

Hamish, knowing they had just moved in, strolled along to welcome them to the village. Dick came as well. "I'm right curious to know what it looks like now," said Dick.

It was a prime location, thought Hamish, facing as

it did the long sea loch. The playground had been dug up and earth put in, ready for a garden.

Hamish rang the bell and waited. The door was jerked open by a tall, mannish woman. "What's up?" she demanded, looking at Hamish's uniform.

"Nothing," said Hamish soothingly. "We just came to welcome you to the village."

"Come in. I suppose you're just nosy and want to poke around like the rest of the people here."

She turned away, expecting him to follow her. But Hamish turned away as well, said to Dick, "Come along. We're wasting our time."

When Mrs. Leigh came back to the door and peered along the waterfront, it was to see the tall figure of Hamish and the smaller figure of Dick heading towards the police station.

She shrugged and went in to join her husband. "Who was that?" he asked.

"The local copper."

"What did he want?"

"Said he wanted to welcome us to the village. Only wanted to nose around like the rest of them. I told him so and he got the huff."

Mr. Frank Leigh was a small, fussy little man with grey hair and a small wrinkled brown face like a walnut.

"For God's sake, Bessie, we don't want to antagonise the local fuzz. Go and apologise."

"Go yourself!"

"All right. It was your idea to move here, so make the best of it. Hand me my stick."

Hamish and Dick were lounging in their deck chairs when Hamish saw a small man struggling to open the front gate.

"It's jammed," he called. "Go round to the side door."

Hamish rose and went into the police station and through to the kitchen. He opened the door and looked down at Frank Leigh. "Can I help you, sir?"

"I'm Frank Leigh."

"And I'm Hamish Macbeth. What can I do for you?"

"I've come to apologise for my wife's rudeness. It's the strain of the removal, you see. The villagers have all been calling and she got fed up. We're only used to city life."

"Come in," said Hamish. "Can I get you something? Coffee? Something stronger?"

"Have you any whisky?"

"Yes, sit yourself down and I'll get you one."

Frank looked around the kitchen and at all the gleaming appliances. "I see you've got all the latest gadgets," he said. "Wouldn't have thought a local copper could afford all this."

"I can't," said Hamish, lifting down a bottle of whisky from a cupboard and thinking, who's the nosy one now? "Dick Fraser, my policeman, is a quiz expert, and he won all this stuff on television shows. How do you take your whisky?"

"Just neat. Aren't you joining me?"

"Daren't risk it in case I'm called out."

Frank downed his whisky in one gulp and looked hungrily at the bottle. Hamish poured him another one.

"So where are you from?" asked Hamish, leaning his lanky form against the kitchen counter.

"London."

"And what brought you up here?"

"Quality of life." Frank seized the bottle and poured himself a full glass.

"A lot of English people come here looking for that," said Hamish, "but the long dark winters get them down and they soon leave."

"Not us. Thish is a nice place."

Hamish guessed he had been drinking earlier. He firmly closed the whisky bottle and put what was left of it back in the cupboard.

"Are you retired?" he asked.

"Yes."

"What was your business?"

"None of yours, copper."

"So that's the end of your chat," said Hamish, a steely note in his voice. He went to the kitchen door and held it open. "My regards to your wife."

Grumbling under his breath, Frank left.

Hamish sighed. He hoped the Leighs would soon get tired of the Highlands and go back to London.

He was just wondering whether to go back to the garden and join Dick when there came a hammering at the kitchen door. He opened it to face Bessie Leigh.

"How dare you!" she yelled.

"How dare I what?"

"How dare you force whisky on my husband? I shall report you to your superiors."

"You do that," said Hamish calmly, "on the understanding that the police will want your whole background and your husband's medical records."

"You…you…," she spluttered. Then she said viciously, "Don't come near us again."

"My pleasure," said Hamish sweetly, and slammed the door in her face.

Bessie Leigh had reached the schoolhouse when an odd-looking dog with blue eyes and a large cat came strolling along the waterfront towards her. As they came alongside her, the cat raised its fur, its yellow eyes blazed, and it let out a long low hiss.

Bessie let out a squawk of alarm, dived in, and shut the door behind her.

Settled once more in the garden after recounting the two visits from the Leighs, Hamish said gloomily, "That pair are trouble."

"Maybe not," said Dick comfortably. "The Highlands

sometimes seem wall-to-wall in alcoholics. We often get newcomers like that. Heavy drinkers can be awfy romantic. Ah, the hills and the heather, and all that. The winter'll see the last of them."

Hamish decided to go to church on Sunday, not because he was particularly religious, but because he sometimes felt like supporting the minister, Mr. Wellington.

To his surprise, he saw the Leighs seated in a pew. Bessie Leigh was sporting a large felt hat, and she was dressed in a new-looking tweed jacket. Dwarfed in her shadow sat her husband.

He received an even bigger surprise to find at the end of the service that the villagers were making their way to the schoolhouse.

"What's going on?" he asked Archie Maclean, the fisherman.

"They've invited us all back for coffee and biscuits," said Archie. "You coming?"

"Not me, I've had a row with her. Drop into the station afterwards, Archie, and tell me what went on."

Archie turned up an hour later. "I could do wi' a dram, Hamish."

"This is a police station, not a pub," grumbled Hamish, but he got the whisky bottle out of the cupboard. "So what was it like?"

"Mean, that's what. Cheap instant coffee and water biscuits wi' cream cheese and nowhere to sit. Mrs. Leigh was queening around as if she was auditioning for a part in *Downton Abbey*. Her man was in the corner reading the Bible."

"Expensive furnishings?"

"Naw. Looked like Ikea in a tartan rash. Plain wood furniture and a tartan carpet and tartan curtains."

"So you thought the whole thing phony?"

"That's it."

"I wonder what they're playing at?" said Hamish slowly.

"Och, the same auld thing. They're playing at being highlanders. Won't last."

And when, after two weeks went by, there was suddenly no sign of the Leighs, that seemed to be the case. The curtains were drawn and no one answered the door.

The fine weather had broken. Ragged black clouds flew in from the Atlantic, bringing squalls of rain. Choppy white waves raced down the loch and sent spurts of spray up from the rocks at the end of the shingly beach. A tall heron perched on one of the rocks with its back to the wind, like a man in a tailcoat, defying the weather.

The piles of earth in the schoolhouse garden slowly turned to mud.

The wind rose to a screaming gale, and with it came torrents of rain.

Rain battered at the windows of the police station. The River Anstey was in full spate, racing higher and higher under the humpbacked bridge.

And then, with one of its usual lightning changes, the weather shifted abruptly, racing off to plague the east and leaving the whitewashed cottages of Lochdubh gleaming in watery sunlight.

By late afternoon, when the sun was already going down, heralding the long dark winter nights to come, Hamish went out for a stroll with his pets.

He was looking dreamily at the loch when a small hand tugged at his regulation jersey. He looked down and saw one of the local children, Rory McVee, staring up at him, his freckles standing out on his white face.

"What is it, sonny?" asked Hamish.

"A foot! A foot!"

"Where?"

"Schoolhouse garden."

"Show me."

Hamish hurried after the boy and then called out, "Wait there!"

He opened the gate and walked into the schoolhouse garden. "At the back!" called Rory.

Hamish told his pets to stay, unhitched a torch from his belt, and walked round the back of the schoolhouse. He shone the torch across the garden. The recent storm had channelled rivers through the earth.

In the beam of his torch he saw a foot in a sensible brogue sticking up.

His heart sank down to his boots. He knew all of a sudden that the Leighs had not left at all.

The whole circus of forensic team, police, and detectives headed by the bane of Hamish's life, Detective Chief Inspector Blair, descended on Lochdubh.

Blair made sure that Hamish was relegated to the sidelines, preferring to listen to gossip about the dead Leighs which his policemen had collected from the villagers. Finally, it transpired that there was only one body, that of Bessie Leigh. Of her husband, there was no sign. Hamish was ordered to take Dick and scour the countryside while a watch was put on all airports, train stations, bus stations, and ports. The Leighs' car was missing, a brand-new Audi.

Hamish decided to search the back roads, stopping at various croft houses to ask if anyone had seen an Audi driving past. He went north, guessing that any fugitive would avoid going south. At Lochinver, a man working in his garden said he had seen an Audi going at great speed past his house the day before, but he said there seemed to be several men in the car. Hamish drove on up the coast, looking always carefully to right and left, sure that the car would be dumped.

Just south of Kinlochbervie, he slammed on the brakes. "Seen something?" asked Dick.

"Over there, on the moor," said Hamish. He started up the engine and swung the Land Rover onto the moor, bumping over tussocks of grass and heather. He stopped beside the Audi and got out. A seagull perched on the bonnet glared at him and flew away.

The car was empty, but the keys were in the ignition. "Better check the trunk," said Hamish.

He sprang the trunk.

Inside was the bound and gagged body of Frank Leigh, his dead face twisted in a rictus of pain.

Blair was furious. This was an important case, and he didn't want this sergeant who had taken the glory away from him so many times having anything to do with it. When he arrived, the first thing he did was to order Hamish back to his police station to write a report.

"I'd swear that wee man was tortured," said Hamish as he drove back to Lochdubh. "What do we know about the Leighs? Nothing at all. Frank Leigh must have information about something that someone wanted."

Maybe whoever had taken him had followed in another car. Blair would try to make sure he didn't get any information. Hamish stopped off on the way and bought a bottle of whisky in the hope that Detective Jimmy Anderson would call on him. Jimmy was a friend and had often passed on information in the past—provided he was lubricated with whisky.

And so it turned out. He had just finished his report when Jimmy arrived, his eyes gleaming in his foxy face as Hamish put the whisky bottle and a glass on the kitchen table.

"It's a mystery," sighed Jimmy when he had downed his first glass. "The house had been ransacked, safe open and empty, hadn't been blown so they must have got the code out of them, and papers strewn everywhere. But among thae papers, there aren't any marriage lines or birth certificates, bankbooks or passports. Maybe the villains took them with them."

"How was Mrs. Leigh killed?" asked Hamish.

"Suffocated. Plastic and duct tape wrapped round and round her head. There may be something else when the full autopsy's been done."

"Vicious and nasty," said Hamish. "They seemed to have come from nowhere but, och, that didnae seem ower-strange. I mean, from time to time English folk come up to settle here, but you know how it is, if the weather doesn't chase them off, the drink will get them. It looks as if the Leighs were villains themselves and had something some gang wanted. There was more than one of them, wasn't there?"

"More than one size of footprint. Guess four men, but it looks as if they might have been wearing forensic boots and the whole place had been wiped clean."

"In a wee village like this," said Hamish, "four men drive up and break in and no one sees a damn thing…"

"No sign of a break-in," said Jimmy. "Either the Leighs thought it was friends or someone held a gun on them."

"Wait a bit," said Hamish, clutching his red hair. "They could have come over the back during the night in a Land Rover or a four-by-four of some sort. Get in by the back door. Decide to take Frank Leigh off and torture him. Take him off over the moors and park. One of the men gets into the Audi and drives off sedately and meets up with them. They put Frank in the Audi and one of the men takes the four-by-four away. Did you see any tracks at the back?"

Jimmy sighed. "We didn't get a chance. The pathologist and the forensic team have been working all day in the garden."

"Let's go now!"

Jimmy took a last swig of whisky and got reluctantly to his feet. "You'd better bed down in the cell tonight," said Hamish. "You've had too much to drink and drive."

"Havers. I tell you, laddie, there's nothing at this time of night on the road to Strathbane but the odd sheep."

Dick, Jimmy, and Hamish put on their forensic suits and boots and made their way to the back of the schoolhouse garden, shining their torches on the muddy ground.

"You see!" said Hamish excitedly. "Tyre tracks going out, just a bit there. The rain probably washed away the rest of the evidence. There's no fence at the back. We won't get any further tracks in the heather. But if they went the way I'm thinking, they may have gone past Angus Macdonald's cottage. We'll go and ask him."

"Thon seer gives me the creeps," said Jimmy. "We'll take your Land Rover. I'm not walking up that steep hill to his cottage."

Angus Macdonald opened the door to them, looking more like one of the minor prophets than ever with his long grey beard and long white gown.

He ushered them into his low-ceilinged parlour. His peat fire was smouldering and sending out puffs of grey smoke.

Hamish explained the reason for their visit.

"You havenae brought me anything," complained the seer, who always expected some sort of gift.

"This is police work, you greedy auld man," snapped Hamish. "You've heard about the murders. Did you see or hear a vehicle passing on..." He swung round to Jimmy. "When do you think Mrs. Leigh was murdered?"

"About two weeks ago at least."

"Well, Angus?"

"It must ha' been about two in the morning," crooned

the seer, closing his eyes. "I sensed black evil and went to the window and looked down the brae. A four-by-four was racing along and turned over the moor, heading down to join the road at the outside o' the village. That would be about fifteen days ago."

"That would be them," said Hamish. "Thanks, Angus."

As they made for the door, Angus said, "Oh, Mr. Anderson. If I were you, I wouldnae drive tonight."

"Why?" demanded Jimmy.

"Something's waiting for you on the Strathbane road."

"What?"

"I cannae see any further."

"Maybe you should sleep here," said Hamish after they had walked back to the police station.

"That police cell bed is as hard as buggery," said Jimmy. "I'm off."

He drove carefully out of the village and up onto the Strathbane road. He had to admit, the seer had scared him. Jimmy stopped the car and lit a cigarette. He was about to drive off again when, with a great rumbling sound, a landslide of mud, heather roots, gorse, grasses, and earth crashed down the road in front of him.

He slowly and carefully turned the car and drove back to the police station.

*   *   *

Dick and Hamish went out to check that no one and no cottage had been caught in the landslide. They were muddy and tired when they got back to the police station.

Jimmy's snores were sounding from the police cell.

Hamish showered and got ready for bed. He was just climbing into bed, followed by his pets, when the phone in the police office began to ring.

He went through to answer it. Liz Bentley's voice came over the line. "He's trying to get in the door. Oh, help me! Help me! Oh, God!" There was the sound of a crash, running feet, a shot, and then silence and the line went dead.

"That must be one o' the most imaginative liars I have ever come across," muttered Hamish and went back to bed.

Chapter Two

☠

It is the penalty of a liar, that should he even tell the truth, he is not listened to.

—*Babylonian Talmud*

Hamish woke the next morning to be immediately plagued by a guilty conscience. What if—just what if—for once in her life, Liz had not been lying?

He dressed hurriedly and woke Jimmy and explained his fears. "You'd better get off up there in case," said Jimmy. "There's not much you can do here. I'll let you know of any developments. And take your animals with you. I don't want to be left alone with them."

Dick was already up. "We may as well have a decent breakfast first," he said. "Think how right cross you'll be to find her lying and you with an empty stomach."

*   *   *

They eventually set off on a sunny morning, bumping and swaying over the heather to circle around the landslide.

On such a day, with the blue mountains soaring up to an azure sky, it was hard to believe that anything had happened to Liz.

They gained the shore road. Even the Atlantic was calm: green near the shore and deep blue further out where cormorants screamed and dived.

Hamish began to feel reassured as they drove into the tiny village of Cromish. A couple of women were chatting outside the village shop. Smoke from peat fires rose lazily into the air.

They parked outside Liz's cottage. "The door's closed," said Dick, "and there's no sign of forced entry."

"So let's knock anyway," said Hamish, "and see if we can stop her lying for once and for all."

They got down from the Land Rover. Hamish stretched and yawned, his hazel eyes surveying the highland scene with pleasure. He knocked at the door and rang the bell.

Silence.

He tried the door handle. It was not locked, and the door swung open easily.

"Miss Bentley?" he called.

No sound but the rising wind soughing through the heather outside.

He pushed open the door to the "best room" and

then to the kitchen-*cum*-living-room. Everything was clean and neat, but both rooms were empty.

He went up the narrow stairs—followed by Dick—to where he guessed he would find small bedrooms under the eaves.

Still no sign of Liz.

But there was something in the very silent atmosphere of the place that was making Hamish's highland sixth sense uneasy.

"Maybe she's at the shop," suggested Dick.

"Let's have another look downstairs first," said Hamish.

He went into the kitchen. "There's the phone on the counter," he said. "Let me think. Say she's been telling the truth. He shoots her. Maybe that shot doesn't kill her. Let's look out the back door."

He opened the door and went out into the windy day, Dick crowding behind him.

The body of Liz Bentley lay in a vegetable patch, the back of her sweater stained with blood.

"We've got a garden crop o' bodies," said Dick and laughed hysterically.

They came in their hordes: police, detectives, pathologist, photographer, and a forensic team followed by the press and headed by Blair, who was determined to make the most of Hamish's delay in calling on the scene of the murder.

Making sure the press were listening, he berated Hamish for not having investigated sooner.

Patiently, Hamish referred him to his earlier report when Liz had first cried wolf and the evidence of the local doctor that Liz had been a habitual liar. Only the arrival of Superintendent Daviot by helicopter shut Blair up. Daviot listened carefully as Hamish explained it all again and said he had not acted negligently, much to Blair's fury, particularly when an unshaven Jimmy Anderson weighed in and said according to the locals, Liz was indeed a liar.

Blair thought quickly. The murder of the Leighs was the more dramatic case. Liz Bentley had no doubt been bumped off by one of the local retarded teuchters up here in peasantville. He persuaded Daviot that it would be a good idea to let Hamish Macbeth investigate this murder while the force concentrated on the Leighs.

To Hamish's relief, the press followed the departing cars. Daviot got into the helicopter and was borne off. Blair left Jimmy Anderson with instructions to keep an eye on Hamish and wait until the forensic team and the pathologist had finished their investigations and report to him.

The wind was howling a shrieking lament. Hamish gave a superstitious shudder. Three people murdered on his vast beat of Sutherland. The pathologist, a man Hamish had not met before, finally came out.

Hamish introduced himself. "I'm Jamie Tavish,"

said the pathologist. He was a tall, grizzled man. "Poor wee lassie."

"Shotgun?" asked Hamish.

"Aye, right in the back. But you'll be getting a full report from the procurator fiscal. Man, I've a thirst. Got any whisky on ye?"

I should have opened a pub instead, thought Hamish. This one's as bad as Jimmy.

But Dick said, "I've got a flask o' brandy for emergencies."

"Hand it over, laddie," said the pathologist. "This is an emergency."

The body was being wheeled out to an ambulance as Tavish glugged down the brandy.

"I'd like a wee keek at the body," said Hamish.

Tavish wiped a hand like a ham across his mouth. "Help yourself."

Hamish signalled to the ambulance men to wait. He approached the body on the gurney and gently unzipped the body bag. He stared down at Liz's dead face. She was dressed in a low-cut floral-patterned blouse. The wind whistled over the body, blowing open the neck of the blouse. Hamish gave a stifled exclamation. On the upper part of the left breast were burn marks, red, round, and circular as if made with a cigarette.

He turned from the body and called to the pathologist to join him. "Look there," urged Hamish. "Those are burn marks. This woman was tortured. She isnae wearing a bra. You can see them plain."

"Och, it's probably the midges," said Tavish. "They can be right awful."

"You'll have to take the body back inside."

"Look here, laddie. I haven't got the time." To Hamish's fury, Tavish strode off to his car, got in, and roared off.

Jimmy appeared at Hamish's side. "Where have you been?" demanded Hamish furiously.

"Went for a pee. What's up?"

"I had a look at the body. There are burn marks on her breasts. She's been tortured. Just like Frank Leigh."

"Can't have anything to do wi' him," said Jimmy.

"I'll need to put in a report. Where did they find that pathologist?"

"He's temporary."

"It needs to be investigated. I want to search that cottage after the forensic boys are finished."

"They'll be ages yet," said Jimmy. "Let's start knocking on a few doors."

"I'll go and get some food," said Dick.

Hamish looked at him impatiently, but Jimmy said, "Good lad. Get some whisky while you're at it."

Heads bent against the gale, Hamish and Jimmy went from door to door to meet with nothing but impatient replies from villagers who had already been questioned by the police. According to all of them, Liz had been a liar who had wasted their time and sympathy too often.

"Let's try Dr. Williams," said Hamish.

The doctor lived in a sandstone Victorian villa on the edge of the village. He was just returning to his home with his dog. "I've heard the news," he said. "Poor woman."

"Can we go inside?" asked Hamish. "We've a few questions."

The doctor led the way into a cluttered living room. The walls were lined with books. A peat fire smouldered on the hearth. The dog, a black Labrador, slumped down on the floor. Fishing rods were stacked in one corner. They sat in battered leather armchairs in front of the fire.

"It's like this," said Hamish. "I had a quick look at the body. Liz Bentley had burn marks on her breasts. Did you know about that?"

"Aye, she came to me the other day, saying it was hot oil spatter from the stove. They looked to me like cigarette burns and I told her so. She began to cry, but she was always crying and lying and I was right tired of her. I gave her some cream and told her to get lost."

"Did anyone see a man calling on her?" asked Jimmy. "Any stranger?"

"Nobody sees anything once the telly is on," said

the doctor. "If someone wanted to see Liz and not get seen, he could get in by the back. Was the lock forced?"

"Didn't seem to be," said Hamish, "but we're going back for a proper look once the forensic team has finished. Before the villagers got wise to her, was she romancing anyone?"

"No one I can think of. We've only two single men here, me and an auld man o' ninety."

"How long had Liz lived in the village?" asked Jimmy.

"Four years."

"That all!" exclaimed Hamish. "Where did she come from?"

"Perth. She's got family there, I gather. Of course, she could have been lying about that as well."

"Let's go," said Jimmy. "They should have finished with the cottage by now."

In another mercurial change of weather, the gale had roared away to the east, leaving the countryside bathed in pale-yellow sunlight.

Dick had set up a card table by the Land Rover. He waved when he saw them and said he had got sandwiches from the village shop and some beer.

"You'll make someone the grand wife," said Jimmy. "Let's eat first, Hamish. Give them time to pack up."

"Let's see what they have to say first," said Hamish.

"They're carrying out boxes of stuff and her computer. I'd have liked a look at that."

"We'll go down to Strathbane when we're finished here and go through it," said Jimmy.

The head of the forensic team was a woman. As she stripped off her overalls and hood, Hamish saw she was quite attractive with curly black hair, large brown eyes, and a generous mouth.

Hamish introduced himself, Dick, and Jimmy. "What have you found?"

"I'm Christine Dalray," she said, "and not much. Whoever did this wiped the whole place clean of fingerprints and cleaned the floor as well."

"I think she had been tortured," said Hamish. "The body has cigarette burns on it. Any signs around of her having been tied up?"

"Hard to tell. Whoever killed her did such a thorough job of cleaning up," said Christine. "Is that beer and sandwiches you have there? I'm famished."

"Help yourself," said Hamish. "Dick aye provides enough for an army."

To Christine's amusement, Dick produced canvas chairs from the Land Rover and set them up round the table and then handed around paper napkins.

"How long have you been on the job?" asked Hamish, covertly admiring Christine's very long legs, displayed to advantage in a pair of tight jeans.

"Only a few weeks. I was in Glasgow when I got

the offer of the job. Evidently Strathbane is famous for sloppy forensic work, and I'm not surprised. The fridges, which should contain samples, were full of beer. They're all part of the Strathbane rugby team, and that seems more important to them than any research. Then it's difficult being a woman. They've played a few nasty tricks on me."

"And how do you cope with that?" asked Hamish curiously. "Report them for sexual harassment?"

"No, I just beat them up."

"What!"

"I've a black belt in karate. It comes in handy."

"And to think I was just beginning to fancy her," mourned Jimmy as they drove south to Strathbane. "The minute she said that about beating them up, I could feel my willie shrinking to the size—"

"Spare us," said Hamish.

"I thought she was a right bonnie lassie," said Dick.

"Ask her out," urged Hamish, who was always hoping that Dick would marry and leave the police station. He felt that Dick's housewifely presence put off any women. Not, he reflected sadly, that he had been very clever in that department. He had cancelled his engagement to Priscilla Halburton-Smythe, daughter of the colonel who ran the Tommel Castle Hotel, because of her sexual coldness, although he could not shake off a recurring dream of a warm and passionate Priscilla.

Then there was Elspeth Grant, once a local reporter, now a well-known television presenter. He had been engaged to her but had broken that off because he thought she was two-timing him. And by the time he realised his mistake, Elspeth was no longer interested.

At police headquarters in Strathbane, Jimmy ordered all the material from Liz's cottage to be brought to them in an interview room, because, as he said, if they had it all out in the detectives' room, Blair would shove his face in.

While Hamish switched on Liz's computer, Dick and Jimmy began to sift through the papers. "Have her nearest and dearest been informed?" he asked. "That is, if she's got any."

"She has a sister and a brother in Perth and they're on their way to the procurator fiscal," said Jimmy. "Then there's a cousin. Very quick check of their whereabouts on the night of the murder and they were all in Perth. The brother, Donald Bentley, is a Wee Free minister, the sister, Mrs. Josie Dunbar, is a pillar of the community, and the cousin is a garage mechanic who was drinking late last night and hadn't the time to get up there."

"She didn't use the computer much," said Hamish. "No e-mails."

"I'm amazed anyone can get on the Internet up there," said Jimmy. "No mobile phone."

"Wait a bit!" cried Dick. "You'll never believe what she had in the bank."

"So go on. Tell us," said Jimmy.

"She had about half a million."

"Maybe the family's rich," said Jimmy.

"Maybe worth killing for," said Hamish. "Who inherits?"

"There's her will in this tin box along with instructions for her funeral," said Dick. "Her brother, the minister, gets the money and the house."

"He's identifying the body," said Jimmy.

"She wrote a lot of letters to the hospital in Strathbane, threatening them all with malpractice," said Hamish. "No letters to sweethearts. No letters to friends."

A policewoman put her head round the door. "The dead woman's relatives are here," she said. "I've put them in interview room number two."

"Right," said Jimmy. "You come with me, Hamish, and Dick, you keep going through this stuff."

The minister, Donald Bentley, did not look as if he were a minister of the Free Presbyterian Church of Scotland, or Wee Free, as the church is usually known. It is a strict religion, but the reverend was small and neat and beautifully tailored, with small features, pale-grey eyes, and patent-leather hair. He had a heavy gold watch on one wrist.

His sister, Mrs. Josie Dunbar, was round and plump

with small eyes almost hidden in creases of fat. Her face was partly shadowed by a large brown velvet hat like a mushroom. Hamish scanned a sheaf of notes which Jimmy had handed to him. Josie was a widow.

"This is a sad business," intoned the minister. His voice was deep and plummy.

Hamish thought that an odd description of a murder.

"She brought it on herself," said Josie.

"How is that?" asked Hamish.

She folded her lips. "I would rather not say."

"For goodness' sakes," said Hamish, exasperated. "Your sister has been cruelly murdered and we need to know as much about her as possible to track down her killer."

"She was a sinner," intoned the minister.

"How?" barked Jimmy.

"She led a licentious life."

Jimmy sighed. "Mr. Bentley, your sister was a virgin. Her life couldn't have been all that wicked."

"I had to banish her from my church. She made Mr. Garse's life a hell on earth."

"Who is Mr. Garse?"

"Our chanter."

"They don't have musical accompaniment," explained Hamish to Jimmy. "A man simply strikes a tuning fork on the pew to start a hymn."

"So how did she make this man's life hell?" asked Jimmy.

"She threw herself at him. She waited outside his house to accost him. She sent him presents."

"We'd better have a talk with this Mr. Garse. Write down his name and address and phone number." Jimmy pushed a pad towards Donald.

While the minister was writing, Jimmy turned to Josie Dunbar. "Did your sister confide in you? Did she say she was frightened of someone?"

"Liz was mad," said Josie. "Even as a wee lassie, she was always fantasising. And she was man-daft."

"It's amazing then that she managed to remain a virgin," commented Hamish.

To Hamish's amazement, Josie threw him a roguish look and said, "She wasnae ever attractive like me. The fellows didn't want it even when she handed it to them on a plate."

Liz was not the only fantasist in the family, reflected Hamish sourly.

The questioning went on, but did not lead them to a single clue.

When the couple had left, Jimmy said, "You'd better get back up to Cromish and see if you can dig anything up, Hamish."

"I'd be better off to Perth," protested Hamish.

"I'll get the Perth police onto things. Off you go, and take Dick with you."

"Let me know if you find out anything about the

Leighs," said Hamish. "I mean, Liz was tortured and Frank Leigh was tortured."

"The two cases can't be connected," said Jimmy. "Off you go."

The village of Cromish was in darkness when Hamish and Dick arrived, the sun having gone down at three in the afternoon. "Where do we start?" complained Hamish. "The police must already have questioned everyone in the village." He let his dog and cat out of the Land Rover.

"We could try the village shop," suggested Dick, "and maybe get something to eat."

"I'm not really hungry," protested Hamish.

"But your beasties could do wi' a bite," said Dick. "Folk might be mair willing to talk if we were buying stuff."

"Meaning, it's you that's hungry again," said Hamish. "All right. Let's go."

While Dick searched the shelves, Hamish approached the counter. Behind it stood a stocky grey-haired woman wearing a flowered overall. "No' the polis again," she complained.

"That's us," said Hamish cheerfully. "You must all have been talking about the murder, and I wondered if any of you had any ideas."

"Well, it wouldnae be any of us," she said. "We're a' decent God-fearing folk here. That poor woman told that many lies. But no one saw any stranger around."

Dick approached the counter with a laden basket. "I see you've got a grand bit o' ham there," he said. "I'll take half a pound. And would you have a bit o' fresh fish for the cat?"

A smile lit up her face. "You're an odd pair o' polis. I can let you have a mackerel."

"That'll do fine," said Dick. "Any incomers we might not have met?"

"There's only Anka. A Pole. She works for me. Anka's a right fine baker, and her baps are the talk o' the Highlands."

"What's she doing up in a remote place like this?" asked Hamish.

She wiped her hand on her apron and held it out. "I'm Sadie Mackay."

"Hamish Macbeth, and this here is Dick Fraser."

"Aye, well, Anka was on a hiking holiday and she ended up here. There's no' that much money to be made in a wee shop like this, although we do have the post office as well. Anka said she was a baker in her father's shop in Warsaw. She said she would bake some stuff for me and sure enough, folk started to come in from all over. She said she was tired o' hiking and took a cottage here, rented it from Joe the fisherman."

"Wait a bit," said Hamish, his hazel eyes sharpening. "You say folk come from all over and yet you say there have been no strangers in the village."

"They come during the day. Liz was killed in the night."

"Any baps left?" asked Dick, who was addicted to those Scottish breakfast rolls.

"Sold out."

"I would like to talk to this Anka," said Hamish. "Is she in the shop?"

"No. She comes in every morning at six o'clock to start baking. But if you turn left, three houses along, you'll find Anka."

Dick paid for the groceries and took them out to the Land Rover. "I'll just get the stove out and brew up some tea," he said.

"No, I want to see this Polish woman. Don't make a face like that. Feed Sonsie and Lugs and I'll go myself."

Hamish found Anka's cottage, but there was no answer to his knock. He pushed a note through the door saying he was parked on the waterfront and would like to speak to her.

Chapter Three

Hamish returned to find that Dick had forgotten the stove and had lit a fire of driftwood. "Kettle will boil soon," he said. "I've made some ham sandwiches."

"What are you going to do with all the other stuff?" asked Hamish.

"I like to keep emergency rations in the car," said Dick. "We might be stuck up here for a bit."

"I left a note for this Anka," said Hamish. "If she doesn't turn up after we've eaten, I'll go and bang on a few doors."

Hamish, Dick, and the dog and cat gathered round the fire, Hamish and Dick sitting on canvas chairs. It was cold and clear with bright stars burning overhead.

Glassy waves curled and crashed on the beach. It

was hard to believe that a vicious murder had taken place in such a quiet setting.

They were just finishing their meal when they were bathed in a greenish light. "Look at that!" cried Dick. The aurora borealis, the northern lights, swirled overhead, like some beautiful sky ballet.

"I never get tired of the sight," said Hamish dreamily. He lay back and stared upwards.

"Did you want to speak to me, Officer?"

Hamish jerked upright as a vision walked into the firelight. "I'm Anka," said the vision.

Hamish had often made jokes about the women in detective stories with high cheekbones, auburn hair, and green eyes, but this was exactly what he found himself looking at.

He stumbled to his feet. The fire blazed and crackled; the green lights danced and swirled overhead. He was never to forget the enchantment of this first sight of Anka Bajorak.

"I did want to ask you some questions," he said.

"Then we'll go to my cottage." She turned away, and Hamish followed.

Dick watched them go with a sour expression on his face. His one fear was that Hamish would get married and that he would have to leave the police station which he regarded as his little palace.

Anka led the way into a small kitchen-*cum*-living-room. She bent down and put a match to the fire, which had been laid ready to light. She was wearing narrow jeans, showing long legs ending in low-heeled ankle boots. Anka took off the scarlet puffa jacket she had on and slung it over the back of a chair.

Hamish tried hard not to stare. Her blue cashmere sweater showed small, high breasts.

Anka took down a bottle of whisky and two glasses. She poured a small tot of Scotch into each glass and handed one to Hamish. Hamish felt he should say he did not drink on duty, but, then, who would know?

She indicated he should sit down at the kitchen table. Hamish raised his glass. "Slainte," he said.

She sat down opposite him and asked, "What is it you want to know?"

Her voice had only a slight accent. The truth is, thought Hamish, I want to know if there is a man in your life. But he said, "What was your impression of Liz?"

"I was very angry with her. She told me her great-grandparents were Polish and were killed during the Warsaw Uprising in World War Two. She said she loved my baking but was so short of money. I gave her a big parcel of cakes and rolls as a present and began to ask her about Poland. I quickly realised that she was lying. Then someone told me she was quite wealthy. Then there was that business when she claimed to have cancer. Such a liar. I avoided her after that."

"I gather from Mrs. Mackay," said Hamish, "that

your baking is so famous, people come from all over to buy stuff. That must bring strangers into the village."

"Yes, but no one strange, if you know what I mean. You know what it's like in the Highlands, everyone knows everyone else. I had some trouble with the men, so Mrs. Mackay told me to stay out of sight and she began to tell visitors that she bakes everything herself."

"Do you know the villagers very well?" asked Hamish. "How long have you been here?"

"I've been here six months. And, yes, it is such a small place, I do know everyone."

"Did you ever hear anyone threatening Liz Bentley?"

"There was a lot of fuss when they found she had tricked them over the cancer business. Someone broke her windows."

"The highlander can be vengeful if he thinks he has been made a fool of," said Hamish.

"But I gather she tricked them two years ago. Surely someone would have retaliated then."

"Not necessarily. Up here, they take their time. Here is my card. If you think of anything, could you phone me?"

"Of course. More whisky?"

Hamish hesitated only a moment. He wanted to stay in her company as long as possible. "Just a small one."

"So what drove you into being a policeman?" she asked.

Hamish looked puzzled. "It's a good job. I get the

station and a bit of land up the back for my sheep. I love Lochdubh."

"But didn't something happen to you in the past that made you want to catch villains?"

Hamish laughed. "Do you mean, do I have a sinister dark side? No, I am just a lazy copper who loves his life most of the time."

"Are you married?"

"No. What about you?"

"I was. I'm divorced now. He turned out to be a drunk and a wife beater. As soon as I got my freedom, I left Poland and went on my travels. I worked in hotels in London for a while and saved money and decided to see more of Britain. I'll maybe go back to Poland soon. Have you any ideas at all about this murder?"

Hamish felt he should be discreet. After all, everyone in the village must be considered a suspect. But as he looked into her green eyes, all he wanted to do was prolong the visit as long as possible. So he told her about Liz having been tortured and about the Leighs and about Liz's phone call and how he did not go immediately because he thought she had been lying.

"The way I see it," he said, "is someone tortured her for some reason, maybe to get information out of her. The burns weren't fresh, so they happened maybe a few days before she was shot. That was when she went to Dr. Williams claiming they were caused by oil spatter."

"So why didn't she phone for help then?" asked Anka.

"Maybe she was too frightened."

Anka gave a shiver. "I've suddenly realised just how awful it all is. The murderer could be right here. What if it is someone mad who will murder again?"

"I don't think so. I'd better go back and take a look at the garden and see if there is any sign that someone drove up to the back of the cottage."

"I'll come with you," said Anka, reaching for her jacket.

Hamish's conscience told him that he should not be taking a civilian with him, but he told his conscience to get lost.

He and Anka ducked under the police tape and made their way round the side of the house to the back. A dark figure was crouched in the garden. Hamish shone his torch and shouted, "Police!"

In the light, he recognised the forensic expert Christine Dalray.

"What are you doing here?" asked Hamish.

"Going over everything again," she said. "I wanted to check out how he got into the cottage with nobody seeing him."

"It was the middle o' the night, after all," said Hamish. "But that's why I am here. Any tyre tracks?"

"The heather at the back is so springy, it wouldn't

hold anything. There are footprints in the garden but they're not much use because whoever it was wore something over their footwear like our forensic boots."

"Just the one person?"

"Maybe more. Who is this?"

"This is a local, Anka. I was questioning her about the villagers."

"Might I have a word with you in private, Hamish?"

"Sure."

"I'll leave you," said Anka quickly.

Hamish sadly watched her go.

"Now," said Christine, "what are you doing involving a villager in the investigation?"

"I need someone who knows the people here to help me," said Hamish defiantly.

"I should report you."

"You don't look the type of lady to do anything so mean."

"Not this time, then. Let's have a look around in the morning. I'm staying down at Kinlochbervie. See you about nine o'clock?"

"Right," said Hamish, "if I can find somewhere to stay. My budget doesn't run to a hotel."

Hamish was often amazed at the amount of stuff Dick managed to pack into the Land Rover. A small tent had been erected near the fire.

"You've been away a long time," complained Dick. "I thought we'd better stay the night."

"Grand," said Hamish happily. With any luck, to-morrow he would see Anka again.

He took off his uniform of sweater and trousers and hung his trousers up in the Land Rover. He crawled into the tent and eased himself into a sleeping bag. Dick followed him, crept into his own sleeping bag, and promptly fell asleep. Sonsie and Lugs lay together at the entrance to the tent. Hamish lay listening to Dick's gentle snores with mounting irritation. The man was making Hamish positively claustrophobic. Hamish considered that Dick was blocking him off from any chance of marriage. He had interfered before. Before he finally fell asleep, Hamish vowed that if Dick came between him and Anka, he would get the pest transferred back to Strathbane.

But it was hard to stay angry with Dick when Hamish woke to the sound of a crackling fire and the smell of brewing tea. He struggled out of the tent in his under wear, stripped off, and plunged into the sea, gasping as the cold waves hit his body. When he came out, it was to find a small group of villagers, standing a little way away, giggling and pointing.

Dick handed Hamish a towel. He dried himself, got dressed, and advanced on his audience, who melted away before he could reach them.

"I'll talk to that lot later," he said, taking a seat by the fire.

"I've made you a bacon bap," said Dick. "Man, thae baps are the best I've ever tasted."

It was a cold, crisp day with sunlight sparkling on the waves. The dog and cat chased each other around the beach like children let out to play. Hamish then ate, and, after fetching a bag from the Land Rover, took out an electric razor and began to shave.

"Christine, the forensic lassie, is coming back at nine o'clock," said Hamish. "But I'll go back to the cottage and have a look at the back in the daylight. Why don't you knock on a few doors and see if anyone remembers anything?"

Anka had finished her baking chores and was considering going to bed when there came a knock at the door. She opened it and found Dick Fraser on the doorstep.

"Not more questions!" said Anka. "I have told Hamish all I can think of."

"Just a wee word," pleaded Dick.

"Oh, all right. Come in. Take a seat. Coffee?"

"Grand. Milk and one sugar, please."

Dick studied her covertly while she made the coffee. Surely there was something suspicious about such a beauty immuring herself in this remote village.

A small television was on the kitchen counter. Anka had been watching the news before Dick had arrived.

"That's Hamish's girlfriend," said Dick.

She swung round. "Where?"

"On the telly. Elspeth Grant."

"Have they been together long?"

"Oh, years. They're just working out the logistics. I mean, Hamish's work is up here and she's down there, in Glasgow."

Anka put a mug of coffee down in front of Dick and then sat opposite.

"Anyway," said Dick, "what I really want to know is can you give me a recipe for thae baps?"

"Is that all you came about?"

"Well, yes. I've never tasted baps like that before."

"I'll think about it."

Meanwhile, Hamish was at the back of Liz's cottage, up on the moorland, painstakingly searching the ground. Yet all the time he searched, he racked his brains for an excuse to see Anka again, and as soon as possible. The trouble with heather, he thought, was that it did not break even when a vehicle went over it. He turned and looked back at the cottage to see Christine taking plaster casts of the footprints in the garden. She waved to him and went on with her work.

I might have fancied her if I hadn't met Anka, thought Hamish. At the top of the braes, he found a discarded cigarette packet and, beside it, the stub of a cigarette. He took out a forensic bag and put both items into it.

Whoever it was, he thought, would stay well clear of the village. He wouldn't want folk to hear the sound of the engine. On the other hand, he could switch off the lights and the engine and cruise down the brae to the back of the garden. Hamish continued on, bent double, searching the ground. If the driver came in a four-by-four, he would circle around over the moorland in a wide arc and join the road well away from the village. He finally hit a boggy patch and saw tyre tracks and hurried back to Christine to tell her to make a cast of them.

"Show me where," said Christine. "I don't hold out much hope. If it were one of those American CSI programmes, I would say, aha, this belongs to a long-wheel-base Discovery Land Rover, or something. But it's not like that, particularly with the team I've got."

"Aren't any of them coming to join you?" asked Hamish.

"Not them. They had a rugby match last night against the Strathbane Diamonds and lost. I phoned up and most of them seemed to have gone off sick, which means monumental hangovers all round."

"And the pathologist is a useless drunk, I think," said Hamish bitterly. He waited while Christine took the cast, and then they walked back up to the top of the brae.

"You can get a good look at the village from here," said Christine.

"Aye," said Hamish, his eyes sharpening as he saw Dick leaving Anka's cottage. "Now, what has that interfering little sod been up to?"

"What?"

"Never mind. I wonder where Jimmy has got to. He's supposed to be here."

"And that's another drunk."

"He's a good detective," protested Hamish, who did not like to hear Jimmy criticised. "I'll leave you now and go talk to a few people."

"Shouldn't take you long," said Christine. "It's more of a hamlet than a village, although there seem to be a good few cars outside the shop."

"That's an example of the great bap hunt," said Hamish. "There's a Polish girl does the baking and they come from all over. Now, there's a thing. They all say that no strangers have been seen in the village. But what about that lot? I'd better get down there."

Jimmy was just arriving when Hamish reached the shop. He had two policemen with him.

Hamish rapidly told him about the fame of the shop's bakery and how it attracted people from all over. "Easy for someone to mingle with the crowd and suss out the place," he said.

But diligent questioning by Jimmy, Hamish, and the police officers only elicited the fact that there had been strangers to the village, but no strangers to the

Highlands. They were told that people from Lochinver and villages north and south of Cromish had all been recognised, which was what Hamish had previously feared.

"How is the investigation into the Leighs' murders going?" Hamish asked Jimmy.

"That's at a dead end," said Jimmy. "Daviot is fretting. He's thinking of sending Blair up here while you go back down there. He says it's your village and you've got a better chance of digging something up than Blair."

"Bad idea," said Hamish quickly. He did not want to leave Cromish and maybe not see Anka again.

"What! I would ha' thought you'd be desperate to get back to your sheep and hens and rural boredom."

"Tell you what," said Hamish, "there's no need for me and Dick to be up here. When you leave, take Dick with you." He told Jimmy about finding the cigarette packet, the discarded cigarette, and the tyre tracks.

"Well, now I'm here," said Jimmy, "I may as well go round the village and see if I can dig up anything. Damn! Where did all those black clouds come from? To add to my misery, it's going to rain. I'll give it the whole day and then I'll take Dick Fraser off with me."

Questions, questions, questions, thought Hamish later that day, and no answers. The wind had risen, sending squalls of lashing rain into his face. Dick had greeted the news that he was returning to Lochdubh with delight. He said he would take Sonsie and Lugs with him.

Hamish waited until Dick was entertaining Jimmy and the policemen with sandwiches and beer from Sophie Mackay's shop and hurried off to see if Anka was at home.

His heart gave a lurch when she opened the door to him. He privately chided himself that he knew nothing really of her character.

"Oh, Hamish," she said. "Come in. Not more questions?"

"Chust wanted to see how you were," said Hamish, the sudden sibilance of his accent showing his nervousness. He reflected that he had rarely seen such beauty outside the pages of a glossy magazine. Of course, Priscilla Halburton-Smythe was beautiful, but there was a generous warmth and sexiness about Anka that was lacking in Priscilla, he thought disloyally.

He followed her into the kitchen. "Do you watch a lot of television?" he asked, indicating the set.

"I keep it on for company. Oh, there's your fiancée."

"What?"

"That news presenter. Your policeman told me you are getting married."

That's it, thought Hamish bitterly. He's got to go.

"I am not engaged to be married to Elspeth or anyone else," he said stiffly. "We were engaged at one time but it didn't work out. I don't know why Dick told you that." Oh, yes, I do, he thought savagely. And I want to deal with that problem, now.

"I've just remembered something," he said. "I'll call later."

He marched back to the camping site where Dick was sitting by the fire. "Where's Jimmy?" demanded Hamish.

"The shop's closed and he wanted whisky so he's gone to Kinlochbervie. He'll be back to take me to Lochdubh."

"And when you're there," said Hamish coldly, "you can start packing and you know why. I've told you before not to interfere in my private life and I'm sick of you."

The rain had stopped, but a high wind was sending ragged clouds flying across the moon. Hamish walked to the beach and stared at the crashing waves, beginning to feel he had been too cruel, and then wondering why.

Dick sat miserably by the fire. He would have to go back to Strathbane and its dirty drug-ridden streets, and leave the paradise that Lochdubh was to him. He heard the noise of a boat's engine coming at speed along the coast. To distract himself from his woes, he raised a powerful pair of binoculars and focussed them on the approaching vessel. It was a powerboat. He registered with alarm that a masked man was at the wheel and another masked man was holding a gun.

Dick hurtled down the beach and flung himself on Hamish and drove him down into the sand as a bullet whined over their heads.

"Keep down," shouted Dick. "Someone's trying to kill you!"

He lay panting on top of Hamish as the boat roared off into the night.

"That was close," he gasped.

They staggered up from the beach in time to meet Jimmy. When he heard the news, he phoned the coast-guard and Strathbane and put out an all-points alert.

"You're a lucky man," he said to Hamish. "Dick saved your life."

"Yes, thanks, Dick," said Hamish, "and let's forget about what I said before." This was followed by an un-charitable thought that if Dick kept saving his life, as he had done before, he'd never get rid of him.

Elspeth Grant sat sulkily in the front of a Winnebago as it headed north from Glasgow on the next day. She had once been a reporter with the local newspaper in Lochdubh, and her connection to Hamish Macbeth was well known to her bosses. So she had been urged to go and do a report on the murders and the attempted murder of Macbeth.

She did not like leaving her job as news presenter

for fear that she might be replaced by someone permanently during her absence. Also, Elspeth told herself, she had got over Hamish and did not want any of her old feelings about him to return to plague her.

Her team consisted of Bertie Andrews, camera, Zak Munro, sound, and Ellie Waters, researcher.

Elspeth had not worked with any of them before. None of them had ever travelled to the very north of Scotland before.

"It's getting dark already," complained Ellie as they stopped in Lochinver for a coffee.

"There's not much daylight in the winter months," said Elspeth. As the first stars began to blaze in the sky over the mountains and ever-restless sea, Elspeth began to feel her spirits lift. There was nowhere more beautiful, she thought, than the northwest coast of Sutherland, where the old people still believed in fairies and that the seals were inhabited by the spirits of the dead.

She wondered whether Hamish was back at his police station or still in Cromish, but she had been ordered to go to the village first and do a colour piece.

As they drove into Cromish, she saw there were police and reporters going from house to house.

"We'll need to wait until daylight to get some shots of the village," complained Bertie.

"Follow me round and get some shots of the locals,"

ordered Elspeth. "There might be someone photo-
genic." She had been thinking along the lines of something like a gnarled old fisherman but certainly nothing
like the beauty that confronted her when Anka opened
her door.

Elspeth's first thought was, first Priscilla, now this.
She could feel her hair frizzing up and wished she
had put on some make-up. She never bothered getting
made up until she was talking to the camera.

"I would like to film an interview with you," said Elspeth after the introductions were over. She knew the
other press probably had shots of a beauty like this,
and she would never be forgiven if she left such a pho-
togenic subject out of her report.

"Very well," said Anka reluctantly. "But as I told the
police, I really don't know anything."

"Just take a few minutes," said Elspeth.

While the cameraman and the soundman got their
equipment ready, she retreated to the van where she
put on make-up with a practised hand, took off her
warm anorak to reveal a pale blue woollen trouser suit
which hugged her figure, slipped on a pair of high
heels, and went out to start the interview.

Anka felt the interview and filming were going to go
on forever. The enthusiasm of the cameraman, Bertie,
seemed to know no bounds. First there was the walking
shot of Elspeth approaching the door. Then Anka invit-
ing her in. This was followed by the interview—first of

how Anka had come to Cromish and then her reaction to the murders.

"You certainly must wish you were back in Poland," said Elspeth hopefully.

"No, I like it here," said Anka. "The murders have nothing to do with me. You see, at first I thought it was some maniac, but now that they have tried to kill Hamish, it means some sort of gang. Drugs, perhaps."

"You know Hamish?" asked Elspeth sharply.

"Oh, yes. We had a nice chat. So gentle and sympathetic. Not like a policeman at all."

"Is he still around the village?" asked Elspeth.

"Mrs. Mackay at the shop says he's been called in to police headquarters. Poor man. He must be in shock."

"He'll survive," said Elspeth curtly. "He's been shot at before. Don't record any of that last conversation, Zak!"

At the end of a long day, Hamish was back at his police station in Lochdubh, but told to go back to Cromish on the following morning. A search for the boat had gone on all around the coast without success. But Hamish's suggestion that maybe the deaths of the Leighs and Liz were somehow tied up was beginning to look as if it might be true.

As he and Dick drove north, a heavy frost glittered in the headlights. The sun was just rising above the mountains when they headed into Cromish, blazing fiery red on the frost covering the houses and heather. Most of the press had left, but there was one television van parked at the waterfront with the Strathclyde Television logo on the side.

A little way away, Hamish saw the all-too-familiar figure of Elspeth doing a piece to camera. She was wearing a power suit with a very short skirt and a pair of stilettos.

She looked across and saw him. A trick of the light made her odd silvery eyes shine red.

"Hamish," she said, approaching him. "Is there anything you can tell me? Why would someone want to kill you?"

"Haven't a clue," said Hamish. His red hair blazed with purple lights in the rising sun.

"Can I do an interview?"

"Elspeth, you know better than that. Strict instructions from headquarters. No interviews."

Dick shuffled his regulation boots. He could not forget that Hamish had nearly married Elspeth. If only all these women would go away, if only the murders would be solved and he could go back to his easy life in the police station.

Sonsie stared at Elspeth, her fur raised, but Lugs ran forward for a pat.

"Have you got anything at all that might help me?" asked Hamish.

"Amazing that no one heard anything at all," said

Elspeth. "I've got enough for a colour piece, including an interview with a very beautiful Polish lady."

"That would be Anka," said Hamish, trying to sound indifferent.

Elspeth looked at him with a certain sadness in her eyes. "Don't get involved, Hamish. You'll get hurt."

Elspeth came from a Gypsy family and often had psychic experiences. Hamish repressed a shudder.

"Well, I'm off after I get into something more comfortable," said Elspeth.

Hamish bent and kissed her on the cheek. She smelled somehow of clean air and heather.

He suddenly wished it could have worked out. But she turned away and disappeared into the van just as Hamish's phone rang.

"'Member me?" said a hoarse voice. "Scully Baird. I ken who tried to kill ye."

Chapter Four

She's as headstrong as an allegory on the banks of the Nile.

—Sheridan

"Who?" demanded Hamish.

"Someone's coming. Meet me in the Wee Man."

"I'm up in Cromish. I can be there in a couple of hours' time."

"Right," said Scully, and rang off.

The Wee Man was an unsavoury pub in the back-streets of Strathbane. Jimmy arrived to hear Hamish's latest news.

"Could be a trap," he said. "You stay here and I'll get someone to pick Scully up and sweat him for a name."

"Won't work," said Hamish. "He'll only talk to me. Scully was in with some really bad drug gangs before he cleaned up his act. I'll go."

"Oh, all right." Jimmy looked round and then leered.

"Also, how you can leave the ladies behind is beyond me."

Elspeth had just emerged from the van in her travelling clothes and Anka stood at the edge of the scene.

Was ever a woman put on this earth to scramble up a man's brains like Anka? thought Hamish. A kitchen goddess who can bake baps and who has the face of an angel.

He turned away to brief Dick but had to wait while Dick unloaded the vast amount of things he thought he might need from the back of the Land Rover.

The weather had changed again as he crested the hill leading down into Strathbane. A greasy drizzle was smearing the windscreen, and low clouds lay over the grimy town.

Hamish had changed into civilian clothes and a disguise. He had posted on a fake moustache and pulled a woollen hat over his flaming hair. He parked the Land Rover outside police headquarters and then set off on foot.

The Wee Man was a squalid pub. He pushed open the door and went into the dark interior, which was punctuated with blue lights from the electronic cigarettes of the customers. Hamish had given up smoking but often craved a cigarette. He wondered if these fake cigarettes were any good. He ordered a tonic water and then looked around but could not see Scully.

Hamish chose a table in the corner where he could see the entrance. Time dragged on. He was about to give up when the door opened and Scully came in. Although Scully was only twenty years old, his previous drug taking had aged him and given him a wasted look. He was very thin with large hands and feet.

"Get me a drink," said Scully, sitting down and pulling a black woollen cap off his head. "Double whisky."

Hamish got it for him, sat down, and said, "Out with it."

Scully took a gulp of his drink. Hamish had found him half-dead of drugs a year ago on one of his rare visits to Strathbane. He had rushed him to hospital, and after he was detoxed had taken him back to Lochdubh and locked him in the cell until he was sure the young man was completely clear. He had then put Scully into rehab.

Scully took a gulp of his drink. "You know the Cameron gang?"

"Aye," said Hamish.

"Well, it was you that led to Cameron being arrested and banged up. But he got out on parole and disappeared. In the gang there's a newcomer, Wayne Forest. Cameron fancies himself a big-time gang boss like in the movies and so he tells this Wayne he has to make his bones."

"You mean Wayne has to kill someone?"

"Aye. For sure. And he's told that someone is you. Cameron sees you're in Cromish from the telly. He pinches a speedboat and gets Wayne a high-powered rifle."

"Where did you hear this?" demanded Hamish sharply. "You're not back on the stuff, are you?"

"Not me. But that lot never could keep their mouths shut."

"But no speedboat was reported missing."

"That's 'cos it was Fergus Fitz's speedboat."

"His rival drug dealer."

"Right."

"Where's Cameron holed up?"

"You know Bevan Mansions?"

"The tower block down at the docks?"

"That's the one. Top floor. Number one hundred and fifty-eight."

"Are you going to need witness protection, Scully?"

"You know how it is. You go into the witness protection and the police aye house you in the equivalent to what you're living in. You live in a slum, so they put you in another slum. I'd best clear off."

"Thanks, Scully. I'll see if I can get you some sort of award."

"Don't," said Scully. "Cameron's got feelers everywhere and I bet that includes the police."

"Okay," said Hamish. "But keep off the booze or I'll have to put you back into rehab."

"Booze isnae drugs."

"Same difference," said Hamish.

By rights, Hamish should have reported to Blair. But instead he called Jimmy.

The first thing Jimmy said was, "Have you told Blair?"

"He'll mess it up. He'll shoot his mouth off all over headquarters and we might have a policeman who's in Cameron's pay."

"Can't get round it, Hamish. Try to report direct to Daviot. Cameron will be armed and we'll need permission for armed police. I'll get down there myself and we'll go in about two in the morning. I'll pick you up at headquarters."

As Hamish entered headquarters, he asked a policeman if Blair was around and heard to his relief that the detective inspector was off sick. Probably a hangover, thought Hamish as he made his way up to Daviot's office.

"He is not to be disturbed," snapped Daviot's secretary, Helen, who loathed Hamish.

"This is a national emergency," said Hamish.

He opened the door to Daviot's office and walked in. The chief superintendent was slumbering in the chair behind his desk.

Hamish went out again and shut the door. Then he banged on it loudly and walked in again.

Daviot was now studying a sheaf of papers. He looked up. "What is the reason for this intrusion, Macbeth? I did ask not to be disturbed."

Hamish put his cap on the desk and sat down, and before Daviot, who expected inferiors to stand in his presence, could complain, he rapidly outlined what he had found out about the attempt on his life.

Daviot began to look excited. "This is wonderful news, Hamish. Has Mr. Blair started organising things?"

"Well, the poor man is off sick," said Hamish. "Anderson is heading back down to arrange everything. We're going in at two in the morning."

"Good, good. Really, this demands a celebration." He pressed a buzzer on his desk and, when Helen came in, asked her to fetch tea and cakes.

The Highlands is the place to be, thought Hamish amused. Any other police station, they'd be pouring out whisky, but up here, it's tea and cakes.

"So that means," said Daviot, "if your informant is correct, the attempt on your life has nothing to do with our murder cases?"

"Seems that way, sir."

"Ah, Helen, what have we here? Eccles cakes! How splendid. I am very partial to Eccles cakes, and Dundee cake, too! My Helen can't be beaten."

"Maybe," said Hamish as Helen deliberately slopped tea into his saucer. "But there's a lassie up in Cromish that bakes baps like baps should be and usually never are."

"Do you hear that, Helen? You must get me some, Hamish."

Helen went out and slammed the door.

"And how is Fraser getting on up there?" asked Daviot.

How Hamish longed to put the boot in and ask that Dick be transferred to Strathbane. Daviot was so happy that he would allow it. But Dick had saved his life.

"Just grand," said Hamish. "Works very hard." Cleaning, polishing, and dusting, he thought bitterly.

"I would suggest, sir," said Hamish as Daviot was about to pick up the phone, "that you arrange the armed squad but do not tell them where they are going or why until the very last minute."

"And why is that?"

"Because one of them might talk to a wife or girl-friend who might talk to her friends and before you know it, news of the raid will be all over Strathbane."

"Just what I was thinking," said Daviot crossly. "You must not try to tell me how to do my job, Macbeth."

Hamish returned to Lochdubh to get an hour's sleep and savour having the place to himself.

He arrived back at police headquarters an hour earlier than he had been instructed to report there. Jimmy had been told to head the raid. Hamish knew that

Jimmy, who sometimes had a fit of what Hamish privately damned as the Blairs, might try to go without him.

Sure enough, they were just setting out. He jumped back into his Land Rover and followed them. Policemen, detectives, and SWAT team members gathered in a vacant lot near the tower block.

"Quietly, lads," said Jimmy. They all spread out, policemen covering back and front entrances of the tower block while the SWAT team went in.

Hamish approached Jimmy. "Were you trying to keep me out of this?"

"Yes, I was," said Jimmy. "It was for your own good. I didn't want one of them trying to kill you."

"Havers," said Hamish bitterly.

The very air around the dismal tower blocks was foul, smelling of sour earth, urine, and beer.

Suddenly they could faintly hear shouts and yells coming from the top of the tower block where Hamish had been told Cameron lived.

He silently prayed that Scully was right.

He heaved a sigh of relief when a handcuffed procession escorted by the SWAT team finally emerged. He recognised Percy Cameron and wondered illogically whether being named Percy had driven him to a life of crime. Three other men were with him, along with a spotty youth.

Jimmy had a quick consultation with the leader of

the SWAT team and then returned to Hamish. Pleased with the success of the raid, Jimmy was now feeling guilty about trying to keep Hamish out of it. "Drive me back, Hamish," he said, "and I'll fill you in."

As they headed back to police headquarters, Jimmy said, "The forensic lot are on their way. Masses of every type of class A drug in that flat and a wee laboratory for making crystal meth. They'll all go away for a long time. Do you want to sit in on the interviews?"

"I'd like to interview Wayne Forest first to make sure he got his orders from Cameron," said Hamish.

"Right," said Jimmy. "I'll arrange it."

But Jimmy experienced a sharp pang of jealousy when they were met by Daviot, saying, "Well done, Hamish. We need more men like you in Strathbane."

Wayne started by demanding a lawyer and was told sharply that under Scots law, he would only get a lawyer when the police decided to let him have one.

He was an unsavoury youth with lank greasy hair and prematurely bent shoulders, probably from slouching from an early age.

Wayne stared at them defiantly as the questioning began in earnest once the preliminaries were over.

"Did Cameron order you to shoot me?" asked Hamish.

Wayne smirked. "No comment."

Hamish was normally a placid, easy-going man. But

he saw red. This useless piece of garbage had caused Dick to save his life, trapping Hamish forever after, amen, in the police station with him.

"You useless piece of shit," roared Hamish. He marched round the desk, picked up Wayne, and slammed him up against the wall.

"It was Cameron. He tellt me tae do it," wailed Wayne, and burst into tears.

Suddenly appalled at his own outburst, Hamish lifted Wayne gently back into his chair and said quietly, "Now be a good wee laddie and write it all down."

Later, when Wayne's confession was secured, and Jimmy and Hamish had retreated to the police canteen, Jimmy said, "It got a good result. But what came over you, man? I've never seen you lose your cool like that before."

Hamish shrugged. "I wanted an end o' it. There are still two murders to solve."

"When we've finished our coffee, we'd best get back downstairs, see what they've got on the Leighs. Then you'd better get back to Cromish," said Jimmy.

But there was very little to learn as there had not been any documents, passports, or credit cards found in the old school. The sale had been handled by an estate agent in Dingwall, employed by Strathbane's schools department. The full amount had been paid by a cheque from a bank in Luxembourg and signed by an H. J. Story. Luxembourg banks were notoriously secretive but had finally told Interpol that the mysterious Mr. Story had cleared out the account and closed it down once the cheque for the sale of the schoolhouse was through. Mr. Story had initially opened the account six months before the sale by depositing two million euros. And for a deposit of two million euros, the bank had not studied his paperwork very closely. They produced a copy of his passport and an address in Luxembourg. Police went to the address to find that Mr. Story had only rented the apartment; there was no sign of him. The apartment was now rented to a couple with three small children and there seemed not to be any hope of getting DNA or fingerprints.

"Daviot's not satisfied," said Jimmy. "He's sending me and Blair over to Luxembourg in a couple of days' time to see if we can dig up anything."

"Once Blair gets his hands on the duty-frees," said Hamish, "you'll probably spend the time coping with him. What about cameras at the bank?"

"They say they destroy the tapes after three months."

"There must be a huge amount of money involved," said Hamish. "Money laundering from drugs or arms sales, maybe. Or some big heist. There have been a lot of jewel robberies in France, in Paris and in Cannes. Millions' worth stolen. Anything there? I don't think there can be any tie-up wi' Cameron. He's too small-time to be in the international league if it turns out to be drugs."

"I think Luxembourg is going to be crowded," said Jimmy. "Interpol is working on it and Scotland Yard are sending experts. Oh, God! What will they make of Blair? Oh, well, off you go. By the way, no one's had time with all this, but you might like to find more about that Anka female. I mean, what's someone who looks as if she came off the catwalk doing up in the back o' beyond?"

"Anyone contacted the Polish police?"

"Haven't had time. I'll get on it when I get back."

"There are Polish people all over the north," said Hamish. "There are the lot who settled after World War Two. Then, thanks to the European Union, the latest influx is so large that the *Inverness Courier* now has an insert in Polish and the Catholic Church had to fly a priest in from Poland. There's the Inverness Polish Association in Albyn House in Union Street. I might drop by tomorrow."

Hamish managed to get two hours' sleep at the station before heading north. It was ten in the morning and a flat disk of a sun had risen low in the sky as if it saw no reason to climb any further, since it would start going down in four hours' time. The previous night's frost was still glittering white on the leaves of the ferns bordering the road. Smoke from chimneys rose straight up into the air.

Hamish's conscience began to trouble him. There had been many opportunities to get married before Dick had moved into the police station. If he really loved Elspeth Grant, then he would move to Glasgow. But, corrected a nasty little voice in his brain, if she loved you, then she would move to the Highlands. Or was it nothing at all to do with Dick, but the fact that there was always part of him that hankered after Priscilla, despite knowing that her sexual coldness would sabotage any hope of a happy marriage?

He thought of Anka and put his foot down on the accelerator. What a beauty! And she could bake!

It was only as Cromish hove into view that he re-alised he should have been worrying about the murder of Liz.

There was no tent on the beach. He asked Mrs. Mackay if she had seen Dick and was told he had taken a room at the doctor's house. He walked up to Dr. Williams's villa and knocked at the door.

A plump woman with a scarf tied around her head opened the door. "You'll be looking for your colleague," she said. "He's ben the hoose, in the kitchen. Doctor's at his surgery if ye'll be wanting him. It's that extension at the side."

"I am Police Sergeant Hamish Macbeth, and you are…?"

"Mrs. Malwhinney. I clean for the doctor."

"Did you know Liz Bentley?"

"Of course. It's a wee village."

"What did you make of her?"

"Poor wee soul."

"You didn't dislike her because o' her lies?"

"I don't think the woman could help it. I got a sister like that ower in Lairg. If she says the sun is shining, I look out o' the window to make sure. Come in. You'll freeze out there."

Hamish removed his cap and followed her into a kitchen that looked as if it had not been changed much since the 1950s. It was stone-flagged with a very high ceiling from which hung a wooden pulley with men's underwear hung up to dry. Shelves with various unmatched plates covered one wall. There was a Belfast sink by the window beside an old green enamelled gas cooker.

"I'll get back to my cleaning," said Mrs. Malwhinney.

Dick, with his sleeves rolled up and wearing a flowered pinafore, was mixing something in a bowl. He looked up when Hamish entered. "I think she's been lying to me," he said.

"Who?"

"Thon Anka. I cannae get my baps to turn out like hers."

"Dick, we've got a murder to solve, or had you forgotten?"

"I thocht I'd wait until you came," said Dick sulkily.

"Well, get your pinny off. We've got work to do. But first, get me a coffee and I'll tell you what happened last night."

"It's instant," said Dick.

"Doesn't matter."

"Right."

While Dick made two mugs of coffee, Hamish told him about the arrest of the drug dealers and how Wayne had admitted that Cameron had told him to "make his bones" by killing Hamish.

"I think Cameron samples too much of his own product, which includes crystal meth. He had a laboratory in that flat of his. We'll need to begin at the beginning," said Hamish. "Now, in Liz's documents, there was a will. Her brother, the minister, gets the lot. But he's got an alibi. What are the usual reasons for murder? Money, obsession, revenge, blackmail. She was tortured. So that means she had something or knew something that her killer wanted."

"Christine Dalray is still up at the house," said Dick.

"We'd better get up there," said Hamish. "Let's go."

He and Dick found a policeman wrapping up the police tape. "I've been ordered back to Strathbane," he said.

They went on into the house. Christine was sitting in the kitchen, gazing into space. She turned her head when they entered. "I keep hoping I'll just find something," she said, "but I can't find anything at all. If it weren't for all these crime documentaries on TV, telling villains how to avoid forensic detection, I would say this was a professional hit. Anyway, I've got to get back on to the Leigh murder."

"I'm surprised you didn't give that one priority," said Hamish.

"I'm a woman, right? And the chauvinist pigs down there don't want me getting any glory. I complained to Daviot so I'm about to pack up here and get back to the Leighs' case."

"I've been thinking," said Hamish, "that if she was tortured, she must have had something the killer wanted. Where would she hide something in this wee cottage?"

"Can't think of anywhere. We looked in the ice trays in the freezer, even in the cereal packets and the sugar. Nothing. Well, I'm off. Good luck. When you're next in Strathbane, give me a ring."

She's very attractive, thought Hamish, watching her leave. But I must see Anka again. There was a niggling question in the back of his brain as to what a beauty like Anka was really doing in this remote spot. The Polish Association was open in the evenings in Inverness. Perhaps he might go there later.

"Let's get started," he said to Dick.

"What are we looking for?" asked Dick, sulky at having been dragged out of the kitchen at the doctor's.

"Anything worth torturing the poor woman for."

"She was a liar, right?" said Dick. "What if she talked about having money under the mattress or jewels hidden away or a stash o' drugs? Someone takes her seriously. She cannae tell the beast anything because she's made it all up. I mean, she had a car. She could ha' taken trips to Strathbane."

"And so she could," agreed Hamish. "But we're going to search this place anyway. You take the downstairs and I'll take the upstairs. Where are Sonsie and Lugs?"

"Chasing seagulls on the beach. Do you want me to...?"

"No. They'll be fine. Get to work."

Although the cottage was only one storey, there were two bedrooms in the attics. One looked unused and was small in size. The other was obviously where Liz had slept.

It was a low-ceilinged room with a double bed and two bedside tables. There was a large Bible on the left-hand table. On the wall was a wooden crucifix depicting Jesus on the cross. Hamish stared at it curiously. Liz's brother would not approve, he thought, the Presbyterians considering all "graven images" beyond the pale. Had she adopted another religion? He opened the Bible. There was a dedication. "To my dear Liz. Walk in the footsteps of Jesus. Barney."

Who was Barney? Hamish made a mental note to phone Liz's brother. There was nothing else in either bedside table, all papers and documents having been taken off to Strathbane. The floor was covered in slippery green linoleum and two violently coloured crocheted rugs. Against one wall was a wardrobe. It contained some drab-looking dresses, an anorak, and a tweed coat.

On the top shelf of the wardrobe were several depressing-looking hats. He took them down and shook them out in the hope that something might fall out, but there was nothing at all. Beside the wardrobe was a chest of drawers containing underwear and tights. The underwear was of the serviceable kind. Nothing exotic. No hint that Liz might have been hoping for an affair.

There was no sign that the house had been searched, the murderer obviously having fled after he had killed Liz. Christine had been looking for anything that might give her DNA. Hamish wondered if it was worth slitting the mattress or taking up the linoleum.

He felt he should ask her brother for his permission. He went outside to get a better signal and called Donald Bentley. He explained the reason for his search.

"If you feel you must," said the minister. "I really feel I did not know my sister at all well. She was always strange."

"Did she attend any other church? Had she found any other religion?"

"I do not know. I assumed she would go to the kirk in Kinlochbervie. Why do you ask?"

"There is a crucifix on the wall of her bedroom."

"What? I find that hard to believe. I am coming up to Cromish tomorrow morning. Her things will need to be cleared out and I will need to see when I can put the house on the market."

"Did she have any close friends in Perth she might have confided in?"

"She had a few friends in my congregation at one time, but they all shrank from her finally because of her behaviour and her lies."

"Did she have a mobile phone?"

"That I do not know."

"There is a Bible presented to her from someone called Barney. Do you know of anyone of that name?"

"No."

Hamish thanked him and rang off. He then phoned Jimmy and asked for a copy of Liz's recent phone calls from the landline to be sent to his iPad before returning to his search.

He tossed aside the duvet and slit the mattress. It turned out to be a waste of time. The linoleum came next. He was able to roll it up without too much effort but underneath there was no sign of anything being hidden under the floorboards.

He put the linoleum back and threw the duvet back on top of the ruined mattress.

He went downstairs and out into the garden. A thick white mist had rolled in from the sea, deadening all sound, blotting out the landscape. He remembered there was a shed at the end of the garden. Inside were the usual garden tools and a wheelbarrow. He searched every nook and cranny, every flower pack. He tipped out a sack of fertiliser and a bin of compost.

At last he gave up. Through the grimy shed window, he could see the mist rolling away. He went out and was about to shut the door when a ray of sunlight shone into the shed. Something up on the low roof glinted and sparkled. He went back in and reached up. Something had been stuck up there with a piece of plasticine. Something was glittering at the edge of it. Putting on his latex gloves, he pulled down the plasticine and carefully cleaned it off.

It was an engagement ring. He took out a magnifying glass. The inscription read, YOURS IN CHRIST.

Chapter Five

He for God only, she for God in him.

—*John Milton*

Hamish carefully put the ring in a forensic bag and went in search of Dick. He found him kneeling on the kitchen floor with his head in a cupboard.

"I've found something," said Hamish. "Come out and hae a look. Put on a pair o' gloves first."

Dick backed out and stood up. Hamish handed him the magnifying glass. "Have a look at the inscription."

Dick whistled. "Now, here's a thing. Do you think she wanted tae be a nun? Bride o' Christ and all that?"

"I don't know much about it but I don't think convents go around presenting women with diamond engagement rings."

He went outside and phoned Donald Bentley again and told him about the ring. "I've never heard of such rubbish," raged the minister. "This smacks of popery. She must have gone mad."

"That's what we hope to find out. You have no idea?"

"Not one. But I will ask my parishioners and let you know tomorrow if I find out anything."

Hamish got his iPad out of the Land Rover and Googled churches in Inverness. He scrolled through them all until he came to one, The Church of the Chosen. He noticed that there was to be Scottish country dancing that evening at eight o'clock.

He phoned up a detective he knew on the Inverness police, Mungo Davidson, and asked him what he knew about the church.

"Not much," was the reply. "Happy-clappy by all reports. Run by a Mr. Alex Brough, Canadian. Never any trouble. Claims he has visions and that the world is going to end next May the first at twelve noon precisely."

"Can't have much of a congregation," said Hamish.

"On the contrary, it's a full house. Services on Sunday, but during the week there are dances and film shows, quizzes, things like that."

Hamish thanked him, rang off, and told Dick about the new church, adding that he would go to Inverness that evening and see what it looked like.

He found the church out on the banks of Loch Ness. It did not look like a church, being a large square wooden hut with the name THE CHURCH OF THE CHOSEN in pink neon lights outside.

Hamish opened the door and walked in as people

were being urged to take their partners for an Eightsome Reel.

"Hey, you!" called a man. "Queenie here hasnae got a partner."

Hamish smiled and joined the set just as the band struck up. The band consisted of two accordionists, two fiddlers, and a man on the drums. They were very good indeed.

When it came Hamish's turn to dance in the middle, he felt quite carried away. He kicked up his lanky legs and shouted, "Hooch!" at the top of his voice. Suddenly the band stopped playing, the dancers stopped dancing.

"What's up?" asked Hamish.

A small, round man in a business suit approached him. He had a round head and very small feet. His brown eyes were sunk in pads of fat, and he was completely bald.

"You are new to us, brother," he said in a Canadian accent. "We only cry with joy when we are praising the Lord, and we dance decorously."

"Are you Mr. Drough?" asked Hamish.

"That I am. But finish the dance and I will explain further."

He gave a signal, and the band struck up again. It was the quietest Eightsome Reel Hamish had ever taken part in. When it was over and the next dance, the Petronella, was announced, Hamish approached Alex Brough.

"Before you begin to explain the workings of your church," said Hamish, "I would like to tell you I am a police sergeant from Lochdubh, and I am investigating the murder of Liz Bentley."

"Let us go outside," said the preacher. "I don't like shouting over the music."

The night was still and very dark. Pink reflections from the neon sign rippled on the black waters of the loch.

"Liz was a valued member of our congregation," said Mr. Brough. "She lived such a distance away but she always attended on the Sabbath. What has her murder to do with me or any of us?"

"She had a copy of the Bible with a note in the flyleaf saying it was from someone called Barney. Do you have anyone of that name amongst your members?"

"We had a Barney Mailer, but he left us a few months ago to go to a job in London."

"Liz also had an engagement ring with the inscription, 'Yours in Christ.' Ring any bells?"

"None whatsoever," said Alex. Something in the firmness of his reply told Hamish he might be lying.

"Now, I gather that you preach that the world is going to end on May the first. What gave you that idea?"

"I saw it in a vision."

"What sort of a vision?"

"A voice came out of a tree."

"And where was this tree?"

"I was here on holiday and I had been walking. Do you see that rowan tree by the loch?"

"Yes."

"I was weary and leaned against it. A voice said, 'Be prepared, I am coming for all of you on May the first.' I saw in a blinding flash that this was where I should set up my church, that this was where I should prepare as many as I could for the afterlife."

"And if May the first comes and goes and we're all here, what do you do then?"

Alex's pitying smile gleamed pink in the light from the neon sign. "Oh, ye of little faith," he said.

"That's me," said Hamish. "I will be checking into your background. And I will be back here on May the first to make sure you aren't planning another Jonestown massacre."

Alex raised his pudgy hands as if in blessing. "I forgive you, my son, for your lack of faith."

"Aye, well, I'm going back indoors to hae a wee word with some folk and see what they think o' this load o' havers."

As Hamish turned away, he could have sworn the preacher mumbled something about putting his views where the sun didn't shine.

When he entered the hall it was to find there was a tea break. People were clustered around a long table laden with sandwiches and cakes. He spotted Queenie, his partner in the Eightsome Reel, and approached her.

He introduced himself and asked if he could have a word with her.

Queenie said she was Queenie Macpherson from Inverness. They moved to a corner of the hall, Queenie clutching a cup of tea and a plate of pink iced cakes. She was a woman in her fifties with dyed black hair and thick glasses, wearing a flowered dress over her plump figure.

"Do you believe that the world is going to end next May?" asked Hamish.

Queenie looked around to make sure no one was listening. "I don't," she said. "But the services are fun. I've a good voice and I'm sometimes asked to do a solo. You should hear me sing 'Amazing Grace.' I think most of us come for the fun. The regular kirks are a bit dreary."

"And is it all free?"

She looked awkward. "Well, it's a right successful church and to join, you pay one hundred pounds a year and get a share certificate. Mr. Brough promises to pay out bonuses."

Hamish scanned the hall. "One hundred pounds is a fair bit o' money. Is there a collection on Sundays?"

"Aye, but it's the church, see. You aye give something."

"Can you point me out someone who actually believes this rubbish?"

"Don't tell her I gave you her name! But you should

have a talk to Josie Alexander ower there. The tall drip o' nothing showing her tits."

And there's one nice Christian description, thought Hamish cynically.

He made his way to Josie, who was standing a little away from the others. She had lank brown hair worn in two pigtails. She was wearing a spangled white top with a plunging neckline and a black velvet skirt. She had slightly protruding eyes in a sallow face and a small pursed mouth.

Hamish introduced himself and, as he saw the band was about to strike up again, asked her if she would step outside for a minute with him. She picked up a mohair stole from a chair, wrapped it around her thin figure, and followed him outside. The wind had got up and the sky above had cleared. Starlight danced in the choppy waters of Loch Ness.

"Do you believe the world is going to end next May?" asked Hamish.

"Oh, yes. Mr. Brough has said so. He had a vision."

"Look here, lassie," said Hamish gently, "haven't you read stories in the newspapers about preachers forecasting the end of the world on such and such a date and then nothing happens?"

"I don't read the newspapers."

"Did you know Liz Bentley?"

"The murdered woman? I talked to her a bit. She was a believer as well."

"She had a ring with the inscription, 'Yours in Christ.' Know anything about that?"

"No!"

"Look here, take my advice and don't give any more money to this crackpot religion."

Josie gave a little gasp and turned and ran back into the church.

Hamish phoned Mungo Davidson. "You'd better get onto this," he said. "I don't want to poach on your patch but listen to this." He told him rapidly all he had learned. "He's conning money out of folk," said Hamish, "and I bet if you look into his background, he's done the same thing before."

"We'll get a search warrant for his accounts," said Mungo, "and yes, we'll check up on him. Do you think it has anything to do with your murder?"

"It could be, if Liz promised money to the church and changed her mind. She liked attention and would tell lies to get it. Maybe she promised to leave everything in her will to the church, changed her mind, and got killed because of it."

"I'll let you know what we find out," said Mungo.

Hamish went to police headquarters, where he typed out a report and left the Bible and ring in the evidence lockers. Then he set out on the long road back to Cromish. It was too late to call in at the Polish Association. He fretted that he should really be in Lochdubh, trying to find out more about the murder of the Leighs. It was on his patch. But somehow his intuition told him that there was a thread connecting Liz's death to the Leighs. He would give it two more days in Cromish.

It was eleven o'clock when he reached the doctor's house. There was a light on in the kitchen, and that was where he found Dick, busy over a mixing bowl.

"You're supposed to be detecting," said Hamish crossly. "Not baking."

"Aye, well, I'm just going to do some scones for the shop. I promised Anka," said Dick.

Hamish felt a pang of jealousy and then told himself he was being silly as he looked at the tubby figure of Dick with his grey moustache and grey hair.

"Also, I found out a good bit about Anka," said Dick. "She's older than she looks. She's forty."

"You're kidding. The lassie hasnac a line on her face."

"No, it's true. And she's been married. She got married to get away from her brute of a father and found she was married to a brute of a husband. She got a divorce, but he wouldnae leave her alone, which is why she fled the country."

"I know. She told me all that."

"I have been doing a bit o' detective work," said Dick. "She went to get me a drink and left her handbag open. I saw her passport and had a wee peek. She's forty, all right."

And I'm thirty-three, thought Hamish. But what does a few years' difference matter?

He told Dick about his visit to the church.

Dick slid a tray of scones into the oven. "Like a coffee?"

"Aye."

"It's instant."

"That'll do fine," said Hamish. "Where are Sonsie and Lugs?"

"They had a big supper at Anka's and they've gone to sleep in my room." I'm losing my pets, thought Hamish. Will I never be rid of this wee man?

"I wouldnae think a kirk like that would give out diamond rings," said Dick. "Here's your coffee."

"That's grand. I don't usually drink coffee this late. But I'm so tired, I'll sleep like the dead."

Dick placed a mug of coffee in front of him. Outside, the wind was beginning to rise again.

"I'm surprised you don't want to go back home," said Dick. "Not like you to leave an unsolved murder on your patch."

"Apart from the fact that Blair would make my life hell, I'd like to give it a couple more days up here, Dick. Let's see what we can find out tomorrow."

But the next morning as he went around the village followed by the dog and cat, it was to find people were thoroughly irritated at being questioned over again. He longed to call on Anka, but knew she would be asleep. His phone rang. It was Jimmy. "We're getting nowhere with the Leighs. Daviot wants you back in Lochdubh, pronto. He's had complaints from the villagers about Blair's bullying. You can leave Dick up there."

After he had rung off, Hamish walked to the thin spit of land beyond the tiny harbour which protected the village from the full force of the Atlantic. Enormous waves were crashing on the shore and seagulls swooped and dived, their calls adding to the restless clamour of the waves.

He realised he had quickly become used to this noise. Lochdubh was protected by its long sea loch and high headland. In the middle of all this tumult and uproar, he thought, no one would hear a car arriving at Liz's cottage, or even a shot.

He went to the village shop and asked Mrs. Mackay if she could remember what the weather had been like on the night Liz was murdered.

"It was right windy during the night," she said. "But you know how quickly the weather changes. It was as calm as anything by the morning."

"How can you remember so clearly?"

"Don't be daft! We don't get murders up here. None of us is likely to forget that night."

Hamish walked out of the shop and made his way back to the doctor's. He roused Dick, who was still asleep, and gave him the news.

"I'm sorry to leave you stranded here," said Hamish.

"Oh, I'll be fine," said Dick. "Maybe when folk get to know me better, they might come up with something."

"I'll need to take the Land Rover, of course," said Hamish. "I'll come and collect you when they give me permission."

A police mobile unit was parked on the waterfront as he drove into Lochdubh.

Daviot was just leaving it as Hamish got down from the Land Rover.

"Ah, Macbeth," he said. "Miss Dalray from forensics is at the schoolhouse. We thought it would be a good idea for her to go over the place again. Go and join her and I hope she may find something."

Hamish nodded and got back into the Land Rover and drove to the police station. He filled his pets' water bowls and gave them canned food, ignoring their sulky glares. Sonsie and Lugs were used to having Dick cook real food for them. Telling them to stay, he went out and walked up to the schoolhouse, breathing in the familiar scents of home: peat smoke, tar, pine, and baking. He was carrying his forensic suit under his arm. He stopped outside the schoolhouse and put it on, then bent down and covered his boots before knocking at the door.

Christine answered it. Hamish, his mind often full of Anka, had forgotten how attractive Christine looked.

"Grand to see you, Hamish," she said. "Watch where you walk. I've been taking up floorboards."

"Found anything?"

"Not so far."

"It's a lot of work for one woman," said Hamish. "Why can't they let you have some helpers?"

"I did. But they were called back. Some drug bust."

"Want me to try the bedrooms while you go on down here?"

"Knock yourself out. You might find something I've missed."

There were four bedrooms upstairs with bathrooms en suite. Apart from the well-appointed bathrooms, not a great deal of money had been spent on the rest. The beds, wardrobes, side tables, dressing tables, and chairs were of the kind bought in cheap chain stores. There were no mattresses or duvets on the beds.

Hamish called downstairs, "Where's all the bedding?"

"Taken to Strathbane and ripped apart," she called.

Hamish sat down at a dressing table in one of the largest of the bedrooms. He ran his hands underneath the counter to see if anything had been taped there. Then he turned and gazed blankly around the room. On the wall between the windows hung a badly executed painting of a Highland glen.

He took it down and studied the back. He took out a clasp knife and ripped off the back. Nothing. But there were similar pictures in all the bedrooms.

He collected the remaining three and began to take them apart. He was about to give up and was looking down dismally at the debris beside his feet when his eye caught a dark little blob of plasticine at the very inside corner of a painting of Bonnie Prince Charlie.

"Christine!" he shouted. "I think I've found something."

She came running up the stairs.

"Did you get my report about what I found at Cromish?" asked Hamish.

"Yes, Jimmy gave me a copy."

"There was a ring in a bit o' plasticine like this. Did you check the other plasticine for fingerprints?"

"No prints at all. Whoever put it there wore gloves."

"Be a good lassie and take this off. I can be a bit clumsy."

"I'll get my camera first."

When Christine returned with her camera, she took several shots of the blob, and then gently prised the plasticine free. "It's gone hard," she said, taking out a thin sharp knife. "I'll just cut it open gently…there!"

They both looked down at a diamond ring. The inscription read, YOURS IN CHRIST.

Chapter Six

☠

The bells of hell go ting-a-ling-a-ling
For you but not for me.

—Military song

"I knew there was a tie-up to Liz's death," said Hamish. "Oh, dear. Do I have to report this to Blair?"

Christine went over to the window and looked down. "Blair isn't here today, but Daviot's just getting into his car." She opened the window and called, "Sir! Hamish has found something."

Daviot came into the schoolhouse and made his way slowly up the stairs. He considered it beneath his dignity to run.

He listened carefully after Hamish had shown him the ring and explained it was the twin of the one he had found in Liz's garden shed.

"Why haven't you put in a report?" demanded Daviot.

"But I did!" exclaimed Hamish.

"I'm sure Mr. Blair would have given it to me if you had."

"Not necessarily, sir."

"What do you mean, Macbeth?"

Hamish opened his mouth to slag off Blair, to point out how many times the man had tried to sabotage his cases, but realised, in time, that all that would happen was that he would get blasted for criticising a senior officer, so he said, "I believe he is busy with a drugs bust and probably has not had the time."

"Anything else I should know?"

Hamish described his visit to the church in Inverness and how Inverness police were going to look into the church's financial records and also find out about Brough's past.

"Well, well," said Daviot. "I shall look into that when I get back to Strathbane. Carry on searching. Give me that ring and the plasticine. You had better return to the lab, Miss Dalray, and check for fingerprints."

"Was anything found out about Anka Bajorak?"

"Nothing criminal. Left Poland to get away from an abusive ex-husband."

When Daviot was back in his office, he asked his secretary, Helen, to find Blair and tell him to report to him immediately.

After five minutes, Blair came in, his face flushed with the previous night's drinking.

"Why did you not inform me of Macbeth's report?" demanded Daviot.

"What report, sir? I did not see any report." Blair had, in fact, torn it up.

"Why should Macbeth lie to me and say he had put in a full report on the Bentley murder and The Church of the Chosen?"

"Covering his scrawny arse as usual."

Downstairs in the detectives' room, Jimmy slung his coat on the back of his chair. Suddenly curious to know what Blair was working on, he went to his desk. Blair's desk was absolutely clear. Jimmy was about to turn away when he saw a sheaf of papers torn in four in Blair's wastepaper basket.

So the old fart was working after all, thought Jimmy. He picked out the papers and saw immediately that it was a report from Hamish Macbeth. He scanned it quickly and then looked round.

"Anyone know where Blair is?"

"Been summoned upstairs to the presence," said Detective Andy MacNab.

Jimmy hurried up the stairs and, ignoring Helen's cry of protest, walked straight into Daviot's office, where Blair and Daviot were companionably drinking tea and eating Tunnock's caramel wafer biscuits.

"I came straight up, sir," said Jimmy, "because I found an important report from Macbeth torn up and in a wastepaper bucket."

Daviot held out an imperious hand. "Let me see it."

Blair lumbered to his feet. "I'll be off then, sir."

"Sit down!" barked Daviot. He pressed a button on his desk, and Helen came hurrying in. "Get me some Scotch tape," ordered Daviot.

When Helen returned with the tape, Jimmy watched as Daviot's manicured fingers neatly stuck the pages together and he then began to read.

A seagull landed on the windowsill and surveyed the scene with one prehistoric eye.

Blair cringed when Daviot eventually raised his head and said in a thin, cold voice, "Where did you find this, Anderson?"

"In Chief Detective Inspector Blair's wastepaper basket."

"Please leave us."

When Jimmy went outside, he saw that Helen was away from her desk, so he pressed his ear to the door.

Blair was blustering, protesting that he would never, ever have done such a thing. "You see, sir, I am afraid the trouble is this. Anderson is after my job. He's deliberately torn up Macbeth's report and put it in my wastepaper basket to make me look bad."

Jimmy marched in again.

"What is it, Anderson? I told you to leave."

"I was waiting to have a wee word with Helen about something," said Jimmy, "and so I heard what Mr. Blair said. I cannae let such a slur on my character go. The solution is simple. All our fingerprints are on file. I have handled the papers and so have you, sir. Mr. Blair says he has not touched them. But the fingerprints of whoever tore the report up will be clearly marked. I suggest they be taken over to the lab."

"This is a waste of police time!" shouted Blair. "Sir, you know me as a good member of the lodge. Have I ever lied to you, sir?"

Daviot hesitated. The fact was, he knew where he was with Blair. Blair always treated him with respect, always remembered to send flowers on the superintendent's wife's birthday. He had a deep resentment towards Hamish, because in a previous case where Mrs. Daviot had been drugged and made to look as if she was having raunchy sex with a villain and Daviot had jumped to the villain's commands in order to stop photographs of his wife appearing in the papers, Hamish had recovered the photos for him and hushed the whole business up—but had kept one photograph which he had threatened to get published if Daviot closed down his police station.

Right at that moment, Hamish entered Daviot's office. Suddenly angry about his missing report, he had raced to Strathbane.

"There is no need to waste the lab's time with fingerprinting," Daviot said to Jimmy. "Macbeth, get Helen to retype your report and give it to me."

"Certainly, sir," said Hamish cheerfully. Daviot knew very little about computers. All Hamish really had to do was go to the computer he had written the report on and print out another copy.

"That will be all," said Daviot.

Helen was furious. "All you need to do," she snapped, "is print out another copy."

"Can't be done," said Hamish cheerfully. "Some numptie wiped it out."

"I'm not doing this for you."

"It's not for me, it's for our boss, but I'll go back in and tell him you're refusing to type it out."

"No, don't do that. I'll do it. Shove off."

He dropped a kiss on the top of her head and went off whistling.

As he drove back to Lochdubh, early darkness was blanketing the countryside. A gale was driving ragged clouds across a small moon.

Six o'clock already, thought Hamish. He wondered if Christine had found any fingerprints on the plasticine or on the ring.

Lights were shining in the schoolhouse when he drove along the waterfront. He parked outside and went in.

Christine was downstairs in the hall, packing up her case.

"Find anything?" asked Hamish.

"Not a thing. I checked out what we found, and there are no fingerprints. I've sent them off to the lab in Aberdeen to see if they can find any DNA. I came back up here in the hope of discovering something, anything."

She stripped off her forensic suit and then sat on the floor and pulled off the covering over her shoes. Christine had a lithe, slim body and small high breasts. Hamish felt low rumblings of lust before pulling himself together and telling his hormones to lie down.

She yawned and ran her fingers through her springy, curly hair. "Gosh, I'm hungry."

"So am I," said Hamish. "Tell you what, I'll take you along to the Italian restaurant and we'll both have something to eat."

"That would be grand. Oh, someone's knocking at the door."

Hamish opened the door and found himself confronted by the Currie sisters. Both were middle-aged, both wearing identical headscarves and camel-hair coats. The light from the doorway glinted on their glasses.

"We want to make sure there's no hanky-panky going on," said Nessie.

"Hanky-panky," echoed the Greek chorus that was her sister, Jessie.

"What on earth are you talking about?" demanded Hamish.

"In there," said Nessie firmly, "is a young and vulnerable woman and we all know your reputation."

"Reputation," mourned Jessie.

Hamish was about to say something very rude when he remembered in time that the Currie sisters were seemingly bottomless funds of gossip.

He stood aside. "You'd better come in and meet her."

He made the introductions and then said, "Before you ladies start blackening my character, I would like to remind you both that a nasty murder has been committed in our village and if you saw anything or if you have heard anything, it is your duty to let me know. And it is no use you looking at Miss Dalray as if she's the whore o' Babylon. She is a forensic scientist and worthy of respect."

The sisters looked at each other in silent communication. Then Nessie said, "I don't think they were married."

As usual, Hamish edited out her sister's echo.

"Why? Did she tell you?"

"We called after they first came."

"This is the Leighs?"

"Them, aye. We took along a cake to say welcome. She invited us in and gave us the worst coffee we've ever tasted. She turned to her man and said, 'Stop sitting there like an idiot, Bert, and take those papers out the back and burn them. Hop to it.'"

"Wait a bit," said Hamish. "His name was Frank."

"That's the point, see. If you can't even remember your man's name, stands to reason you're not married to him. I said that I thought Mr. Leigh's name was Frank and herself said that Bert was her pet name for him. Have you ever heard such havers?"

"That's interesting," said Hamish. "Anything else?"

"No, but we'd like a wee word with Miss Dalray."

"Not now. Shoo." Hamish urged them towards the door.

Nessie turned on the doorstep. "Remember what it says in Corinthians, Miss Dalray. 'It is better to marry than to burn.'"

Jessie's voice echoed back to them. "Burn."

"What was that all about?" asked Christine.

"The village guardians of my morals," said Hamish. "They go around swearing I am some sort of Casanova."

"And are you?"

"No such luck. Let's eat."

Willie Lamont, the waiter in the restaurant, had once been a policeman, but had married the restaurant owner's daughter.

"You're a bit early," he said.

"A problem with that?" asked Hamish.

"No, we're aye ready." Willie whipped a can of

spray cleaner from behind his back and liberally sprayed the table and then began scrubbing it with a cloth. "This is called Goaway," he said proudly. "It'll remove anything."

"You've just taken the polish off the table," said Hamish.

Willie squawked in distress. "It's not supposed to do that."

Hamish seized the can from him. "You daft gowk. It says on the label, 'Do not use on wood.'"

"It's my eyes," mourned Willie. "I hae the stigma."

"Do you mean astigmatism?" asked Hamish.

"Something like that."

"Well, do the other thing it says on the can. It says it removes everything, so remove yourself and bring us a couple of menus."

"But I'll need to take the table away to resurface it."

"Willie!"

"All right. I'm going. Miss Halburton-Smythe is back. Will she be joining you?"

"No. Menus."

"Who's Miss Halburton-Smythe?" asked Christina.

"Just a friend."

"But Willie had a malicious look on his face when he asked if she'd be joining us."

"I was engaged to Priscilla at one time. I do not want to talk about it. Willie was being nasty because I wouldn't let him take the table away. He's passionate about cleaning."

Willie came back and gave them two leather-bound menus.

"Will you be needing to use protection?" he asked Christine.

"What!"

Hamish leapt to his feet, his face scarlet. "How dare you!"

Willie backed off. "What did I say wrong? It was that telly star, Luke McBain, what was in here the other day. I says to him, I says, 'Would you like an aperitif?' and himself says, 'It is not called an aperitif. It is called protection that we need to use against the damn cold up here.' So I thought I was being unsofacated by calling it an aperitif."

Christine began to laugh. "I thought you were selling condoms."

"Oh, no," said Willie earnestly. "But there's a machine in the toilet."

Hamish sank down in his chair. "Go away, Willie, and leave us in peace to study the menu."

When Willie had left, Christine said, "I wondered why you had never married. I don't think anyone in this village would give you a chance to court anyone. Are they all like that?"

"No, the rest are quite sane. Do you think that perhaps the Leighs were not married?"

"I doubt very much if their name even was Leigh. There's no record of them anywhere under the names they were using. And is Dick Fraser still in Cromish?"

"Yes, choose something and let's talk about it."

They decided to have the same, starting with Parma ham and melon, followed by stuffed peppers. Christine suggested the house red as a choice of wine.

After Willie had taken their order, Christine looked out of the window. A wheelie bin was being blown along the waterfront, chased by one of the villagers.

"It's quite a storm," she said. "Do you believe in global warming?"

"I've not decided," said Hamish. "There's been awful weather before. I watched a documentary on the great storm of seventeen hundred and three. Thousands killed and a hurricane that lasted several days. That was followed by a mini ice age."

"It's grim up here in winter," said Christine. "Don't you ever get weary of it?"

"No, never," said Hamish.

They ate and talked companionably, Hamish mourning the changed days of policing.

"I always seem to be fighting to keep my police station," he said. "They think they could run it from Strathbane, but who would look after the old people in the winter and make sure they had enough fuel and food? That's nearly as important as tracking down criminals."

"Morale is pretty low in Strathbane," said Christine.

"Police are being encouraged to spy on each other. Harry Wilkins, one of the old coppers, was with a new chap and they pulled over a man for having a broken taillight. Now, normally, Harry would have told the man to drive to a garage in the morning and get it fixed, but the new chap is one of Blair's creeps, so he had to tell the man his car was being impounded."

"What a waste of police time," mourned Hamish. "They look on me as a sort of dinosaur."

Christine smiled at him and reached across the table and took his hand. "Not you, Hamish."

"Am I interrupting something?" Neither had noticed Jimmy Anderson coming into the restaurant. Christine snatched her hand back.

Jimmy pulled up a chair. "Hey, Willie!" he shouted. "A double whisky."

"Not if you're driving," called Willie.

"I'm staying the night at the police station, so hop to it."

In an odd way, Hamish was glad of the interruption to what had seemed, moments ago, the beginning of a romantic evening. His thoughts flew to Anka. Lucky Dick to be up there where he could visit her.

"There have been big developments," said Jimmy. "You can call Dick back."

"I'll do that. What's new?"

"A full report from the Mounties in Toronto. Alex Brough skipped Canada before he could be charged with fraud. But there's more. His real name is Peter Gaunt. His partners in crime were a Bert and Bessie Southern, real names of the Leighs, all of them English. They had conned five wealthy residents out of their life savings. The children and relatives of the ones who were cheated have all been checked, and not one of them has left Canada in the past year."

"So what does Peter Gaunt have to say for himself?" asked Hamish.

"He's disappeared. Somehow he must have got involved in something bigger than cheating his congregation or he would have run for it after the murder of the Southerns."

"Unless he was the one who murdered them," said Hamish. "Why were the police so slow at picking him up?"

"They were still going through the church's books when this report from Canada arrived. They sent a squad to the church to find it empty."

"They all must have been into something very big," said Christine.

"Say some big gang had a heist and wanted it out of Canada," suggested Hamish. "There's Gaunt with a false passport and a way to get out of the country and over here. He and the Southerns split up and they take the loot. They disappear. Maybe they've told some villains that they are going to South America—anywhere but the wilds of Scotland.

"But some gang catches up with the Southerns and tortures them to try to find out where the goods are."

"But what about Liz Bentley?" asked Christine.

"I'm slipping," mourned Hamish. "I should have shown her photograph to members of the congregation. There was that ring hidden in her shed. Those rings were maybe a way of anyone involved to identify each other."

"I'll get Inverness police working on that in the morning," said Jimmy, stifling a yawn.

The wind shrieked outside, and there was a crash as a loose piece of board struck the window outside.

"You can't sleep at the police station tonight," said Hamish. "Christine can't drive back in a storm like this."

"It's all right," said Christine. "I've got a sleeping bag in my car and the keys to the Leighs' place. I still think of them as the Leighs. I can bed down there for the night."

"Won't do," said Hamish. "There's a sofa in the living room. Jimmy can sleep in the cell and you can take the sofa."

"I'll be okay," said Christine. She knew there was still water and electricity in the old schoolhouse and she did not want Hamish to see her in her serviceable pyjamas and without her make-up on.

Despite Hamish's protests, Christine insisted on staying at the schoolhouse.

Back at the police station, Hamish phoned Dick and told him the latest news.

"I should stay here," protested Dick. "What about the Bentley murder?"

"Wait a minute." Hamish turned to Jimmy. "Dick thinks he ought to stay up there and keep looking into Liz's murder."

"Oh, all right. Tell him to give it a few more days," said Jimmy.

"You can stay on for a bit," said Hamish. He then told Dick about the report from the Mounties. "Liz must have known someone connected with the church or gone there herself," said Hamish. "See what you can find out."

"What was that about?" asked Anka when Dick had rung off. He told her and then said ruefully, "I've been working more at the baking than the policing."

They were working in Anka's kitchen, preparing the bakery for the morning.

Anka looked at Dick with affection. He had a dab of flour on his nose, and his tubby figure was wrapped in one of her large white aprons.

"I don't think you're cut out for the police force," she said. "I think you would rather be doing this."

I'd rather be doing anything with you than anything else in the whole wide world, thought Dick, but he just smiled and said, "I think our scones are ready."

"Maybe I should have a look around Liz's cottage," said Anka. "I might just see something you missed."

"I'm sure it's against regulations," said Dick cautiously. "But her brother will be up here soon again to check on things now the place is up for sale. It would be grand if we could find just one clue."

"Good. That's settled. We will go tomorrow afternoon. We must have our beauty sleep."

Christine tossed and turned in her sleeping bag, amazed at how frightened of the storm she had become. The noise had moved from a high eldritch screech to a deep bang, bang, bang as if giants up in the sky were slamming doors. She crawled out of her sleeping bag and switched on the light. Nothing happened. Must be a power cut, she thought miserably. I am not brave, but I'm brave enough to admit it. I'm going to the nice safe sofa in Hamish's police station.

She had not bothered to undress. Christine put on her coat and opened the front door, which was nearly whipped out of her hand by the force of the gale.

By dint of hanging on to garden fences, she made her way to the station and banged on the kitchen door.

It was doubtful whether Hamish would have heard her had not Lugs awakened him by barking sharply. Sonsie slid off the bed and went to the kitchen door and stood on guard, fur raised.

Hamish opened the door and let Christine in. "I've

decided your sofa would be better. Wait a bit. You've got electricity. There's a power cut at the schoolhouse."

"I'll make you up a bed on the sofa," said Hamish. "Maybe I'd better go to the schoolhouse and have a look."

"If you bring my sleeping bag, it'll save you looking out bedding," said Christine. "I'll make myself a cup of tea and wait for you."

The roaring wind at Hamish's back propelled him along to the schoolhouse. The front door was swinging open, banging against the outside wall.

He unhitched a powerful torch from his belt and made his way to the living room.

He shone the torch on the sleeping bag and then backed off with an exclamation of alarm. What had been Christine's sleeping bag was shot to ribbons.

There was no sleep for anyone that night as the whole forensic team headed by Daviot and Blair arrived from Strathbane. It was initially decided that shots from something like a Kalashnikov had ripped into the sleeping bag. Whoever had done it had assumed Christine was still inside.

As usual, Hamish was sidelined by Blair and told to interview the locals. Instead, he went along to the Italian restaurant, knocked at the kitchen door, and asked the beautiful Lucia, Willie Lamont's wife, for a cup of coffee. He then sat down at a table in the empty restaurant to think.

Behind all this was big money that some gang wanted to get its hands on. They wanted to scare any investigation away from the schoolhouse, he thought, and then decided that if that were the case, the shooting had the opposite effect. The police would now take the building apart.

Money came from bank robberies, jewel thefts, drugs, arms, human trafficking, and prostitution. The northwest of Scotland with its many small bays and inlets was ideal territory for smuggling.

The weak link was Liz Bentley. Somehow she had become involved. It might be an idea to go back to Cromish and investigate that end further.

He finished his coffee and went out again to the waterfront to be consulted by Mrs. Wellington, the minister's wife. The storm had died and pale sunlight was glittering on the choppy waters of the sea loch. As usual, Mrs. Wellington was encased in tweed. Even her large hat was made of tweed.

"This place has become Chicago," she boomed. "And what are you doing about it?"

"What I can," said Hamish mildly. "Have you heard o' something in Inverness called The Church of the Chosen?"

She sniffed. "That lot. Load of rubbish."

"How did you hear of it?"

"Ellie Noble, thon silly lassie, went there. Her parents came to Mr. Wellington for help. They were afraid it was some sort of cult."

"That's the Nobles out on the Braikie road?"

"That's them."

"And does Ellie live with them?"

"No, she works in First supermarket in Strathbane and I think she shares digs with a couple of girls."

"Thanks," said Hamish and hurried to the police station. He fished out a photograph of Liz Bentley that he had in his desk. It was a print of one given to the police by her brother.

He collected the dog and cat and got into the Land Rover. Blair was just emerging from a police unit set up on the waterfront. He shouted something as Hamish drove past.

Hamish drove on, glancing in the rearview mirror as the image of angry Blair dwindled into the distance.

Chapter Seven

Woman, a pleasing but a short-lived flower,
Too soft for business and too weak for power:
A wife in bondage, or neglected maid;
Despised, if ugly; if she's fair, betrayed.

—Mary Leapor

Hamish knew he was poaching on Strathbane's territory, but he did not care. Knocking on doors in Lochdubh to find out if anyone had seen or heard anything was a waste of effort, he knew. The noise of the storm would drown any car arriving in the village in the middle of the night.

Before leaving the police station, he had changed into civilian clothes, not wanting to attract any attention from Strathbane's police force.

In other towns and cities, supermarkets are often large palaces of goods and clothes, but First supermarket in Strathbane was as dismal as the run-down town itself. Very few people seemed to put their shopping trolleys back in the places designated for them, leaving them strewn instead around the car park. A chilly wind with the metallic smell of approaching snow whipped rubbish around Hamish's ankles as he made for the main entrance. It was situated in one of the poorest parts of the town and dubbed by the locals as Salmonella Centre.

Obesity was a bad problem in Strathbane as illustrated by a large woman at the customer services desk. She looked about as welcoming as Jabba the Hutt.

"Whatdeyewant?" she demanded languidly, raising her eyes from a film magazine.

"I would like to speak to Ellie Noble."

"Ellie Noble! Report to the customer services desk," she roared into a microphone, and then went back to reading her magazine.

The automatic grimy glass doors behind which Hamish was standing opened and closed, sending in blasts of arctic air. As he watched, little pellets of hard snow began to swirl down outside.

A small girl wearing the green-and-red overalls sported by the staff came hurrying up.

"Police," said Hamish. "Is there somewhere we can talk?"

The spots on her face stood out red. "They were throwing the stuff out anyway," she said. "I'm no' going to prison for that."

"I want you to look at a photograph," said Hamish patiently, "and tell me if you recognise the woman."

Colour returned to her face. "We can go to the caff ower there," she said.

Hamish collected cups of coffee for them at the self-service desk in the café and led her to a table by the window.

Ellie had a peculiar figure, thin on top and very broad at the hips.

"It's like this," began Hamish. "I believe you used to attend The Church of the Chosen."

"Went to a few dances there wi' ma mates."

Hamish took out a photo of Liz Bentley. "Do you recognise this woman?"

"That's the one that got herself killt."

"It is. But do you remember seeing her at the church?"

"Aye, it is her. I said as much to my friend Beryl. She was sweet on the preacher. Oh, I remember now. She was flashing an engagement ring around and saying she'd just got engaged. Someone congratulated Mr. Brough, but he said it wasnae him. He led Liz outside. When she came back, she looked as if she'd been crying and she wasnae wearing the ring. This Liz woman told a lot of lies. She'd already told everyone her great-granny was a Russian princess so we thought it was just another of her stories."

"Why did young people like you go all the way to this church?"

"The dances were great and there were a lot of fellows from Inverness went there."

"See any sign of drugs?"

Ellie looked out at the swirling snow. "Maybe," she said in a small voice.

"I'm not here to arrest you," said Hamish. "But it would be a great help if you could let me know what you saw."

"My pal, Beryl Gregg, wanted me to try uppers. Said if you went to the ladies' toilet, you could get them there. I was feart and didnae go."

"Did your friend?"

"Just the once. Then someone told her that the police had their eye on the place so we never went back."

"I'd like to speak to Beryl. Where can I find her?"

"I'll get her. She works here. I've got to get back to work. I'll tell her to see you."

Hamish sat and waited, watching the swirls and eddies of the snow out in the car park where rubbish flew up into the white air. He hoped Beryl would hurry up. He did not want a passing policeman to see his police Land Rover in the car park.

"You wanted to see me?" asked a nervous little voice.

"Sit down, Beryl," said Hamish. "Now, there's nothing to worry about. I just want some information. It concerns this woman."

Beryl was plump, her uniform strained across large breasts. She had a round pasty face and pale-grey eyes.

She looked at the photograph of Lizzie and nodded. "That's her."

"I am not interested in drugs," said Hamish, "only in this woman. Did you ever talk to her?"

"Just the once. I was feeling low and I'm always on a diet, see, and someone said that uppers made you lively and you would lose a lot of weight. You're not going to arrest me!"

"No. Go on. You are being very helpful."

"A lad told me you could get drugs in the toilets so I went to the ladies' and waited. Liz came in and asked what I wanted and I told her. She gave me some pills and told me if I ever said something to anyone, they'd come after me. Well, Liz had become a bit of a joke with all her lies and she was acting as if she was some mafia moll. I told her to stuff her drugs up her fat arse."

"I would like you to make a statement."

"I cannae!" wailed Beryl. "What will my mum say?"

"Look, all I want you to say is you went to the toilet and Liz offered you drugs and you told her to get lost. Can you do that?"

"I s'ppose so."

"Get your coat and tell your boss you are off on important police business."

When the statement was secured, Hamish drove her back to the supermarket. "It's a bad storm," said Beryl. "I hope they close early."

Hamish left her at the door of the supermarket and

drove off. His pets shifted restlessly in the back. He knew if he let them out for a run, it would mean wasting time picking snowballs off their fur at the police station, a job that Dick would have performed. He wondered how Dick was getting on and envied him being up there with the gorgeous Anka.

"Well, we shifted last night's baking just in time," said Dick. "But is there any point in doing anything for to-morrow? The roads will be blocked."

"We can bake a few things for the locals," said Anka.

They were sitting in Liz Bentley's house after having searched it thoroughly without finding anything of interest.

"Do you ever get tired of policing?" asked Anka.

"Sometimes," said Dick. "I know Hamish wants the police station to himself."

"Why?"

"He hopes to get married and he thinks I queer his pitch."

"Queer?"

"I mean, he thinks I get in the way."

Anka laughed. "He is worried the ladies prefer you to him."

"What woman would prefer me to Hamish?" said Dick gloomily.

"Quite a lot, I should think. Kindness and decency are very important."

Dick blushed. Then he said, "Maybe I'm not cut out for police work. Police work means I'm lazy. I don't like asking people questions and often getting doors slammed in my face."

"Have you ever thought of becoming a baker?"

"No' really. I'm too old to change."

"One is never too old," said Anka. "Now, my dream would be to open a bakery in Inverness. Think of it, Dick. We could be famous."

"We?"

"Why not? I have some money left to me by an aunt. I have never touched it."

The wind screeched round the cottage. The trouble with being a policeman, thought Dick, was that you ended up not trusting anyone. Why on earth would this beautiful woman want to go into business with him?

"Why me?" he asked.

"Because like me, you have baking in the blood," said Anka. "And because we have become very dear friends."

Outside, the storm raged on, but somewhere deep inside Dick there was a warm glow, like sunshine.

"Just maybe it might work," he said cautiously. "I've got a fair bit of money put by. I've earned a lot with television quizzes over the years. The last time I won a new car and sold it and kept using my old one."

"Let's go to my place where it is warm," said Anka.

*   *   *

At the mobile police unit in Lochdubh, Hamish handed Jimmy a copy of Beryl's statement, glad that Blair was nowhere in sight.

"So that's the tie-up," said Jimmy. "Say Brough or whatever he calls himself managed to get the drugs out of Canada for some gang with the help of the Southerns, and the gang starts to come after them all."

"I think Peter Gaunt, alias Brough, must be the kingpin," said Hamish, "or he would be dead by now."

"He may be dead for all we know," said Jimmy. "There's not much any of us can do until this storm is over."

"Well, I've got to get on my snowshoes and see everyone in the outlying crofts is all right. Coming with me?"

"You must be mad! The funeral's in a couple of days' time."

"They've released Liz's body?"

"Aye. She's being burnt at the crematorium in Strathbane. Her brother's furious, but Liz left instructions in her will."

"Odd thing for a fantasist like her," commented Hamish. "I would have thought she would want the telly-type funeral with the churchyard and all that."

"No, it's ashes to ashes for our Liz."

Hamish looked out the window of the mobile home. "It's easing off. I barely made it here from Strathbane."

*　　*　　*

Hamish returned to the police station and found to his relief that the phones were working. They often went out of order during a storm. He was therefore able to phone everyone he could think of who might be at risk instead of having to go and visit them.

The police station was cold. He switched on the central heating and lit the stove in the kitchen. As he was cooking up food for Sonsie and Lugs, he reflected that all these little chores were usually done by Dick. When he had fed the animals, he made himself a ham sandwich and a cup of coffee and went through to the living room. The fire was full of cold ashes, and there was a thin layer of dust on the furniture. He retreated to the kitchen and sat down at the table.

He took out his mobile phone and called Jimmy. "I forgot to ask you," said Hamish, "but is there any chance any of the villagers saw or heard anything?"

"Not a thing. They all say that the wind was so awful, it would block out any noise. I've just had a bollocking from Blair and I am told to keep you out of Strathbane in future."

"That man's a right misery. He'll probably confront Beryl and Ellie and shout at them so much they'll clam up completely. I suppose it's all right if I turn up at the funeral?" said Hamish.

"I don't see that Blair can object. Liz was murdered on your patch. If Dick hasn't got anything, call him back. The minute the roads are clear, you'll both need

to go round the village again just in case someone forgot to tell us something."

After he had finished the call to Jimmy, Hamish
phoned Dick at the doctor's house. The cleaner answered and said, "He's ower at the Polish woman's."

Hamish found Anka's phone number and rang her.
"Is Dick there?" he asked.

"Yes, I'll get him," said Anka. "Dick, my dear, it's
for you."

My dear, thought Hamish with a stab of jealousy.

When Dick came on the phone, he said, "The storm
was so bad I had to spend the night here."

"Lucky you," said Hamish tartly. "As soon as the
road's clear, you're to come back here." He told Dick
about the attempt on Christine's life and what they had
found out about the real identities of Brough and the
Leighs.

Dick rang off and said to Anka, "I've been called back."

"The roads haven't been gritted yet," said Anka,
looking at his downcast face.

"The snow's stopped," said Dick, "and it's melting.
I suppose it's back to the real world."

"Why?" asked Anka. "What if we pool our re-
sources and open a bakery somewhere. Inverness is
expensive. What about Braikie?"

"You mean…you and me?"

"Why not?"

"There is already a bakery in Braikie," said Dick. "It was bought last year by some woman who's made a bad job of it. Maybe she'd be glad to sell."

"As soon as we can leave," said Anka, "we will go to Braikie and see what we can find out."

"But even if I hand in my notice," said Dick, "it'll take at least a month until I get my freedom."

"You are ill, that's it!" cried Anka. "I know, I will appeal to Dr. Williams for a certificate."

"You'll be asking the man to lie?"

"Why not? He issues sick notes every Monday to the locals complaining of bad backs when he knows there is nothing up with them."

Hamish was just wondering if his budget would run to a meal at the Italian restaurant when the kitchen door opened and Priscilla Halburton-Smythe walked in.

The first thing she said was, "I see Dick isn't around."

"Obviously," said Hamish.

"I mean, no smells of cooking or sounds of television. Dishes in the sink instead of the dishwasher. You look like a man whose wife has just walked out on him."

"And to think for a moment I was glad to see you," said Hamish. "I gather the road is clear."

"Yes, and the snow is melting."

"How long are you up here for?" asked Hamish.

"Just a few days. Have you eaten yet?"

"Not yet."

"I'll treat you to a meal at the Italians'."

Over dinner, Hamish rediscovered that Priscilla was a good listener. He was able to go over the case in detail.

When he had finished, Priscilla said, "Why try to kill Christine?"

"If this man, Gaunt, is behind it all, then he probably was afraid there was still some incriminating clue in that house that she might find."

"It would have been more sensible to shoot you. Surely you have proved to be more of a danger at finding out things."

"Someone may have seen the lights in the school-house and thought it was me. Something Gaunt or someone else wants badly is hidden and they still don't know where."

"What about this Polish woman, Anka? Don't you think it odd that she should choose to hide herself away in Cromish?"

"I did at first, but she's been checked and double-checked. Dick is still in Cromish, but he'll be back tomorrow."

"You must miss all the home comforts."

"I wish I could get rid of the man," said Hamish. "I want my police station back."

"So what is your next move?" asked Priscilla.

How beautiful she looked, with the golden bell of

her hair shining in the candlelight, thought Hamish. And how contained and passionless.

He said, "I had better go back to Strathbane whether Jimmy likes it or not, and talk to those two girls who used to go to the church. If Liz had claimed to be engaged and it wasn't to Gaunt, who else was hanging around there?"

Hamish's phone rang. To his surprise, the caller was Anka. "I am afraid Dick will not be able to travel," she said. "He has a severe cold. I am taking him to the doctor tomorrow."

Hamish felt a pang of unease. What did he really know of Anka?

"I'll get up there tomorrow to see him," said Hamish.

"That will not be necessary," said Anka and rang off.

"That's odd," said Hamish, tucking his phone back into his pocket. "Anka has just told me that Dick is not well enough to travel. I said I'd go up there, and she told me sharply that it wouldn't be necessary. I don't like this one bit. I'll get up there first thing tomorrow."

"Do you want me to come with you?"

"It's not allowed. You know that."

"We could go in my car," said Priscilla.

"All right, then. I'd be glad of the company."

Hamish reflected, the next morning, that it was comfortable that he no longer lusted after Priscilla. Of course, it was hard to have any passionate feelings for a woman who did not put out one little vibe.

It was a dismal day with a greasy drizzle smearing the windscreen. Priscilla's Range Rover splashed through lakes of melting snow.

By the time they reached Cromish, a gusty wind had started to blow and the sky was clearing to the west.

"What a noisy place," commented Priscilla when they got down from the car outside Anka's cottage. "There must be more seagulls here than anywhere else in the northwest."

"It's the waves as well," said Hamish. "The Atlantic waves get higher and stronger every year."

He rang the doorbell.

"The curtains are closed," said Priscilla. "Maybe she's still asleep."

Hamish tried the door. "It's open," he said. He walked in, calling, "Anka!"

He opened the door to the living room. The first thing he saw was Dick asleep on the sofa.

"Don't wake him!" said an imperious voice behind him. Hamish swung round. Anka was standing there in men's pyjamas. "And who is this?" she said, turning round to confront Priscilla, who had just entered the room behind her.

Hamish made the introductions. Then he said, "Dick doesn't look ill."

"He has seen the doctor this morning and we have a certificate to show you."

What on earth is going on here, wondered Hamish. Has she drugged him?

He stepped forward and shook Dick awake.

Dick blinked owlishly up at Hamish. "I'm sick," he said.

"You don't look it." Hamish put a hand on Dick's forehead. "You don't even have a temperature."

"It is no use," said Anka. "We had better tell them. Let us all go into the kitchen and have coffee."

"It's like this," said Dick. "I am leaving the police. Anka and me are going to start our own bakery, maybe in Braikie."

Hamish stared at him. Here was the news he had longed for. But Dick and Anka. He shot a covert look at Anka from under his long lashes. Even in those pyjamas, she looked seductive from her tousled hair to her bare feet. Such a woman could have any man she wanted. Why Dick? Money, that must be it. She wanted her own bakery, and no doubt Dick had money in the bank.

"Who's going to pay for all this?" demanded Hamish.

"I have my own money and Dick will help out," said Anka. "We are a team. We are superb bakers." She put an arm around Dick, who was sitting next to her. "This man is an angel."

Dick smiled at her. He looked radiant.

"We have so many plans to make," said Anka. "Please give Dick two more days. We have so many things to do."

"If I could just be having a wee word with Dick in private," said Hamish stiffly.

"We'll go ben," said Dick.

In the living room, Hamish confronted Dick. "Look, are you sure she isn't just using you?"

"It might be hard for you to understand," said Dick, "but we are a match when it comes to the baking. This is a dream. Because she's beautiful, you think she can't fancy me. Well, she does. You can't stop me."

"Dick, I'm only worried about you."

"You've been trying to get rid of me for ages," said Dick. "So shove off and enjoy your own company."

"There's no need to be rude. And you are speaking to a superior officer."

"Shove off, *sir*," said Dick.

They glared at each other and then Hamish began to laugh.

"I swear to God I'm jealous," he said. "You've always been more interested in the kitchen than any police work. You can start right away. I'll swear blind you've had a breakdown and tell them that the accommodating doctor has given you a sick note."

"Well," said Priscilla on the road back. "Doesn't that make you feel warm all over?"

"It worries me a bit. She's glamorous enough to break Dick's heart."

"Oh, Dick's attractive."

"Dick!"

"Yes, he's sort of cuddly."

Hamish experienced that nasty stab of jealousy again. For the cool Priscilla to find Dick attractive was really annoying.

He dropped Priscilla at the hotel, almost relieved to see her go. She seemed to epitomise his failure to find a lasting relationship.

Hamish attended the funeral at the crematorium in Strathbane.

The Reverend Donald Bentley gave a frosty eulogy and hoped his sister would be forgiven for her many sins.

There was no one else to say anything about the dear departed.

The crematorium was run by two elderly brothers, Kenneth and Robert Wright. They were identical twins. Both were in their early eighties.

After the last dreary hymn was over, Hamish went to talk to Kenneth Wright.

"Did you know Miss Bentley?" he asked.

"I met her the once," said Kenneth. "That man from that peculiar church brought her along to a service."

"Who was being cremated?"

"A Mrs. Jessica Andrews. It was a most undignified service, I thought. Everyone clapping and stamping to songs I had never heard before. Jesus is your buddy, that sort of thing."

"Could you find an address for Mrs. Andrews?"

"Come into the office."

The office was dark and bleak. A shelf of urns stood against the window.

"I hope those aren't full," said Hamish.

"No, no, no," said Kenneth. "We keep them there as an example of what can be bought."

"You should dust them," said Hamish. "They look a bit dingy, and that one the left has a sair dunt in it."

"Do you want this address or not?" snapped Kenneth. "I haven't got all day."

"Right," said Hamish. "Didn't mean to offend you."

No computer for the Wright brothers, thought Hamish, as Kenneth opened an old-fashioned ledger.

"Ah, here it is. Number five, Loan Road, Beauly."

"Thanks. Are you all right? You look worried."

"I am very well, thank you. Now, if there is nothing else?"

Hamish found Jimmy standing outside the crematorium, smoking.

"You didn't attend the service," said Hamish.

"Slept in. Anyone there interesting?"

Hamish told him about Jessica Andrews. "I might

nip down to Beauly and have a word wi' her," he said.

"Not on your beat, Hamish."

"I know, but there's something else." He told Jimmy about Dick leaving the force and setting up as a baker with Anka. "I think I'd better check in with the Polish society in Inverness, just to see if I can find out anything about her."

"Believe me, Hamish, her background has been checked every step of the way. She's just what she says she is."

"Let me go down there," wheedled Hamish. "You know I can often get things out of people that other policemen can't."

"Oh, all right. But go in plainclothes and if Inverness police catch you, I know nothing about it."

On seeing Beauly, Mary Queen of Scots is reported to have said, "*C'est un beau lieu*" (it's a beautiful place), and so the town came to be called Beauly.

Beauly is near Inverness. It boasts a wide main street and a ruined priory, now the possession of Lord Lovat.

Number 5, Loan Road, was a trim Victorian granite villa. Hamish hoped that some relative of the dead Jessie Andrews still lived there. The front garden was simply gravel, bordered by a stone wall.

There was a polished brass doorbell set into the

wall. The orange glow from the streetlamp outside shone on blank empty windows at the front. Hamish rang the bell.

At first he thought there was no one at home, but then a light went on in the hall inside. The door opened. A small, waif-like woman stood there. She had very fine straight white hair which hung down in two wings beside her thin white face. Although her neck was wrinkled, her face was smooth. She was wearing a faded black sweater and jeans and two large fluffy slippers in the shape of pink bunny rabbits.

Hamish introduced himself and said he was investigating The Church of the Chosen.

"Come in," she said. "I am Jessie's sister, Heather Green."

Hamish followed her small, thin figure to a kitchen at the back of the house.

It was very cold. The kitchen was old-fashioned with a Belfast sink and an old gas stove and a table covered in oilcloth and surrounded by four hard-backed chairs. There was no refrigerator or washing machine.

"Will you take tea, Sergeant?" asked Heather in a high thin voice.

"That would be grand."

She lit a gas ring and put a battered kettle of water on it. Hamish waited until the tea was made and served before he began to question her. Heather clasped her hands round her mug of tea as if for warmth.

"Jessie was a widow," she said. "We lived here together. Jessie inherited quite a bit of money after her husband died. She said she'd made out a will leaving everything to me. And that she did. But apart from this house, Jessie only had fifty pounds left in her bank account. I found out she had been making donations to that church. I confronted that preacher, Brough, and he told me that she had been very generous. He would pay for the funeral but that was all. Our bank manager told me that Jessica had paid the church money amounting to seven hundred and fifty thousand pounds.

"I am a retired schoolteacher. I have my pension, but it's not all that much."

"Can't you sell this house?"

"I suppose I must. But I was brought up here. I never married. I would hate to leave the place."

"What did Jessie tell you about the church?"

"That's what was so odd. She told me nothing until nearly the end. She said she was visiting friends in Inverness. And she had begun to behave oddly. She had always been a placid body. But she began to lose weight and chatter, chatter, chatter."

Drugs, thought Hamish bleakly.

"So how did you hear about Brough?" he asked.

"She said she was going to get married to him and two days later she was dead. The procurator fiscal said it was caused by an overdose of pure heroin. He put 'heart attack' on the death certificate, to be kind. I went to the police. I told them that this man, Brough, had supplied my sister with drugs. They got back to me and said they could find no proof and that Brough had told them he had never proposed marriage to Jessie. I had to let him pay for the funeral because I have so little, you see."

"I believe there are benefits for people in your position," said Hamish awkwardly.

"I could never lower myself to scrounge on the state," she said firmly.

Hamish got to his feet. "If I find anything out, I'll let you know. What is your telephone number?"

A thin flush suffused her face. "I don't have one," she said in a low voice.

Hamish wondered as he drove into Inverness whether Jessie had been murdered. But how to prove it? From her sister's description of her behaviour, Jessie had been taking amphetamines. It would be assumed she had progressed to harder drugs.

He parked in Inverness and made his way to the headquarters of the Polish Association in Union Street. It transpired that Anka had only visited once. Her beauty had made her memorable, but nothing more was known about her.

He collected his Land Rover and drove out to the

church. He fed Sonsie and Lugs with carry-outs he had collected in Inverness and let them run around.

There were great mounds of earth piled up around the church, showing where the police had dug up the property looking for hidden cash and drugs.

There was police tape crisscrossed across the front of the church door. Hamish had a sudden longing to look inside. Hoping it would be put down to vandals, he broke the tape, and, taking out a ring of skeleton keys, fiddled with the locks for half an hour before he got the door open. He shone a torch around the church. Was there anywhere that the police might not have looked? There was evidence that the floorboards had been taken up. Behind the plain altar was a large statue of Christ, not on the cross, but with his arms outstretched in blessing.

Hamish let the light of the torch run up and down the statue. At first sight, it appeared to be made of bronze. But one of the bare toes was chipped, revealing that it was made of plaster. Then he concentrated on the neck. Jesus was wearing a broad metal band around his neck.

Hamish found a chair, stood up on it, and changed his large torch for a pencil torch which he gripped between his teeth. There was a button at the back of the metal collar. He pressed it and the head fell forward on tiny hinges. He shone the torch down into the statue. It was stuffed with banknotes.

Chapter Eight

☠

Money is the root of all evil.

—*Proverbs*

Hamish telephoned Jimmy. He said as he'd been in Inverness, he thought he would drive past the church. He lied and said he'd noticed the tape had been broken and had decided to enter the church and make sure there were no signs of vandalism. He said it was then that he had noticed something strange about the neck of the statue and so had found the money.

Jimmy said he would alert Inverness police and would be there himself as quickly as possible.

Hamish sat down on the steps of the altar to wait.

His thoughts turned to Heather Green. He wished he could take piles of money from the statue and give it to her.

Soon he heard the sound of approaching police sirens.

Mungo Davidson entered the church. "Come outside, Hamish," he called. "We'll let SOCO do their work first."

A team of white-suited scenes of crimes operatives came in. Hamish went outside with Mungo and told him why he had examined the statue.

"Good work," said Mungo. "We never thought to look there. Seemed sort of sacrilegious."

Hamish told him about Heather Green. "I bet a lot of that money really belongs to her. Is there any way when the dust has settled that she could get it?"

"Well, if Brough or whatever he's calling himself is found and brought to trial, he cannot benefit from his crimes. It's a tricky one. How's my dear friend, Detective Chief Inspector Blair?"

"With any luck, he's as drunk as a skunk by now," said Hamish.

"Lovely man."

A cold wind was blowing off Loch Ness.

"Where's that legendary sidekick of yours?" asked Mungo.

"Dick Fraser is leaving the force."

"Pity. From what I hear," said Mungo, "he'd have had a table out and dinner served while we wait. Let's sit in my car and put the heater on."

Hamish whistled and Sonsie and Lugs came running up.

"Thon cat's like a tiger," said Mungo nervously.

"I'll put them back in the Land Rover."

*   *   *

Jimmy arrived, but with only Detective Andy MacNab, not wanting to bring a larger squad to poach on Inverness's territory.

They all sat in Mungo's car. Jimmy bemoaned the loss of Dick and said his mouth was dry with lack of whisky.

Several hours later, they were told they could go back into the church.

Hamish was superstitiously relieved that they had not found it necessary to break the statue but had laid it down and fished out the money through the neck. Neat bundles of fifty-pound notes lay piled up on the altar like offerings to Mammon.

"How much?" asked Mungo.

"About two million," said the head of the forensic team. "We've dusted the notes for fingerprints, but whoever stashed them was wearing gloves."

"Whoever tortured and killed the Southerns and Liz Bentley must have been trying to find out where the money was," said Hamish, "although that puzzles me. It's only about two million."

"And that's not enough for a killing, Mr. Rockefeller?" said Jimmy.

"Not these days," said Hamish. "There's no sign of drugs. This is the money Peter Gaunt, alias Brough, conned out of women. Much of it comes from a woman called Jessie Andrews and should by rights have gone

to her sister. They were dealing drugs in this church.
I swear there's a stash of drugs worth a great fortune
stashed somewhere."

Mungo said, "We'll keep a watch on the church.
We won't tell the newspapers about the find. If Gaunt
needs money, he may try to come back for it."

Hamish got wearily back to the police station by ten
o'clock the following morning just as a winter sun was
rising over the mountains.

But of course there was no longer any Dick to welcome him with a hot breakfast and coffee.

He undressed and got into bed. Before he fell
asleep, he wondered if Gaunt were really the master-
mind or simply a con artist who had been used by
some gang. And what about the diamond rings? Had
they been given to people who knew about the drugs?
He was sure it was drugs.

In late afternoon, he took the dog and cat out for
a walk. The sun had already set and the pitiless stars
of Sutherland shone down on the deep black waters of
the sea loch.

He was joined by Angela Brodie, the doctor's wife.
"Has your man been treating anyone lately for drug ad-
diction?" asked Hamish.

"Not that I know of," said Angela, "but he wouldn't
necessarily tell me. Do you think drugs are behind
these terrible murders?"

"Somehow, I'm sure of it. Where would you go if you were on the run?"

"If I were still after a cache of drugs, I'd stay hidden in Scotland," said Angela. "If I were a villain, then I would go to some remote croft house and hold up the family to let me stay as long as I felt necessary."

Hamish stared at her blankly. Then he said, "I should have thought of that."

"I was up at the Tommel Castle Hotel for dinner last night," said Angela. "Priscilla was dining with some French fellow."

"I thought she was only up on a flying visit," said Hamish. "Who is this French fellow?"

"I don't know. Why don't you ask her?"

"Because she'll think I'm jealous and I'm not," said Hamish huffily.

But later that evening, he decided to go up to the hotel. Not that he meant to spy on Priscilla, he told himself, only just to run the latest discovery past her.

The Tommel Castle Hotel was one of those castles built in the nineteenth century after Queen Victoria had made the Highlands fashionable. It was built on the lines of a French château, complete with turrets.

The manager, Mr. Johnson, hailed Hamish as he entered the reception area.

"Priscilla here?"

"She's dining with a Monsieur Dubois."

"And who is this Dubois?"

"Just a tourist."

"Here for the fishing?"

"No, he says his family came originally from Scotland and he is tracing his roots."

"Oh, the famous Clan Dubois," said Hamish cynically. "I'd like a look at him."

"Now, then. You can't barge in and bother my guests. Wait until dinner is over and ask Priscilla. She's been going around with him."

"I'll have a word with Clarry," said Hamish and made his way to the hotel kitchen, reflecting that he had now lost three policemen to the food business: Clarry to the hotel, Willie to the Italian restaurant, and now Dick to a bakery.

Clarry welcomed Hamish and asked, "Where are the dog and cat?"

"Outside."

"Bring them in by the kitchen door. I've some nice fish for Sonsie and a bit of venison stew for Lugs."

After Hamish had collected his pets, he asked Clarry, "Know anything about this Frenchman, Dubois?"

"Came a couple of days ago. Staff say he's a generous tipper."

"Which part of France is he from?"

"Don't know. Ask Priscilla. Herself has been spending a lot of time with him."

"Let me know when they leave the dining room?"

"Aye. Pablo!" he called to one of the waiters. "Let me know when Dubois has gone up to his room.

"Staff are mostly foreign now," mourned Clarry. "It's all the immigrants from the European Union. Take any job that's going while the lazy sods in the Highlands wake up to find it's hard to get any work at all. Have some dinner while you wait. I've a rare bit o' poached salmon."

They talked of old times while Hamish ate and his animals slept at his feet. At last Pablo came in to say that Dubois had gone up to his room and Miss Halburton-Smythe was checking the stocks in the bar.

"Leave Sonsie and Lugs wi' me," said Clarry. "Shame to wake them."

Hamish stood at the entrance to the bar. The lights of the bar were shining on Priscilla's fair hair. She was talking to the barman. Guests sat around having after-dinner coffees and drinks. There was a murmur of quiet conversation.

When Colonel Halburton-Smythe had fallen on hard times, it had been Hamish who had suggested he turn his home into a hotel. With an excellent manager, the colonel had little to do with the running of the successful hotel but enjoyed dining out at friends' houses to brag about "his" brilliant idea.

A log fire crackled on the hearth. Hamish had a

weak moment in which he wished he were one of the guests on holiday and never would have to worry about murder or mayhem.

Priscilla saw him and came round the bar to greet him. "What brings you, Hamish?"

"I've heard reports of a certain Frenchman called Dubois. I'm interested in any foreigners in the area."

"We've had Germans and Dutch and Spanish here and you've never bothered before."

"I bothered now because o' thae nasty murders."

"Let's sit down over there," said Priscilla. "Oh, well, his name is Paul Dubois. He's a wine merchant. His grandmother was a Mackay. He's interested in his family background."

"Where in France is he from?"

"Lyon."

"Has he asked you for any money?"

"What a question, Hamish! He's a real gent. Are you jealous?"

"That's vanity," snapped Hamish. Then he said, "Sorry. This case has been getting to me. I'll take myself off."

"Do that," said Priscilla coldly.

He collected his pets and drove back to the police station, feeling tired and grumpy. But not jealous!

Annie MacDougal sat in the kitchen of her croft house perched on the foothills of the mountains between

Kinlochbervie and Cromish, and wondered what more the Good Lord could send down to punish her.

Her son and daughter had been killed in a car crash on the A-9 thirty years ago. Neither of them had married and so she had no grandchildren. Her husband had died of a heart attack shortly after the death of the children. Now in her eighties, she had become solitary and bitter and friendless. She had allowed a neighbour to use her croft land, but she never spoke to him.

Now she was facing a man with a gun, a man who told her he would not harm her as long as she kept quiet and made his meals.

Annie did as she was told, all the time eyeing that gun as she would a venomous snake.

Her captor was Peter Gaunt, reduced in size from the dapper man Hamish had met at the church. He had been camping out and was now desperate for warmth, comfort, and cooked meals.

He had watched Annie's remote cottage carefully and noted that she was old and alone.

He took out a fat wallet and peeled off five hundred pounds and handed the money to her. "What we'll do," he said, "is you will drive that wreck of your car down to the shops. I will be in the backseat. If you alert anybody, I will shoot you in the spine. Got it?"

Annie nodded. "I'll get my coat," she said. "I have to go to the toilet first."

"Don't take all day about it and I'll be right outside."

Annie stumbled into the bathroom and sank down on her knees. She could not pray to the God who had let her down so many times. But she believed in the fairies. Fairies, to the old people of the Highlands, were not glittery things but small dark men. Had she not put out milk for them every day? So she prayed passionately to the King of the Fairies for deliverance.

"Are you going to be in there all day?" shouted Peter.

"Coming!" She heaved herself to her feet.

They were just about to leave when there was a knock at the door.

"Open it and get rid of whoever it is," whispered Peter.

Annie opened the door. A small dark man stood there, little more than a dwarf. He had blue tattoos on his cheeks and thick black hair. His eyes were as black as coals. In an odd accent, he shouted, "Peter!"

Peter emerged. "Come with me," said the little man, and without a backwards glance, Peter walked off with him.

Annie rushed back into the house. She had no doubt at all that her prayer had been heard and that the King of the Fairies had sent a messenger to get rid of the horrible man.

*   *   *

Two days later, Mrs. Mackay in Cromish said to Dick, "There's a real odd story going around about the fairies rescuing a woman."

Dick loved a gossip, so he leaned up against the counter of the shop and prepared to listen. "It's this old woman, Annie MacDougal, lives way up in the hills between there and Cromish. Never usually talks to a soul. But yesterday, she was a bit tipsy and she speaks to her nearest neighbour for the first time in years. She says a man held her up with a gun and said he was going to stay with her, so she prayed to the King o' the Fairies for deliverance and he sent a wee man to take the villain away."

Dick thought about the story later and phoned Hamish. "What do you think?" he asked when he had finished.

"I was always worried that our missing Peter Gaunt would try to hole up somewhere remote," said Hamish. "I'll take a run up there and talk to her."

Hamish cursed the long, dark winter nights as he stood outside Annie's cottage and looked around. Although it was only three in the afternoon, it was already dark. Huge boulders left behind when the glaciers had retreated stood in the fields like so many humpbacked men. The wind moaned through the heather.

He knew that a belief in fairies existed in the Highlands and islands. The Macdonalds of Dunvegan still claimed that their flag had been given to them by the fairies. The fairies were reported to be an erratic people, sometimes helping in time of need but often stealing children from cradles and playing malicious tricks. They lived underground in grassy knolls.

He knocked at the door. Annie opened it and looked him up and down, noticing his uniform, and thinking bleakly that the last time a policeman had called it was to tell her of the death of her children.

Hamish removed his cap. "May I come in? There's nothing wrong. I just happened to hear your story of a gunman."

Annie nodded her head and stood aside to let him enter. She wished now that she had not spent some of that money on whisky and so told the tale to her neighbour.

They sat down in hard-backed chairs on either side of the peat fire.

"I don't know that I should talk about it," she said. "The fairies might not want me to say anything."

Hamish thought, with some amusement, that Annie was lucky he was highland. Blair, who hailed from Glasgow, would have damned her as certifiable.

"I'm sure they won't mind," he said soothingly. "It must have been an awful experience."

But she began to talk about all the things that had happened to her in her life, all the tragedies and how God had not listened to her prayers. Everything was so quick these days, thought Hamish. Annie belonged to the pre-television era when everyone told long stories and everyone else listened. The asthmatic old clock on the mantel had chimed out the passing of an hour before Annie got to the visit of the gunman.

Hamish interrupted to ask for a description. It sounded like Peter Gaunt. When she got to the bit about her prayer to the King of the Fairies, her sharp eyes scanned his face looking for signs of ridicule, but found none. When she got to the visit from the "fairy," Hamish longed to ask her what nationality she thought the man might be, and then realised it would be useless. If he took her to Strathbane to use a sketch artist or the new identikit programme on the computer, he would be asked to report what he was doing.

Then he remembered there was a clever artist in Lochinver called Malcolm Douglas. Malcolm mostly painted landscapes, but in the summer he augmented his income by drawing portraits of the tourists.

Hamish explained carefully how he would like to get a likeness of the gunman. At first she protested.

"Come on," said Hamish. "It would be the grand outing and I will take you for dinner in Lochinver." Annie could barely remember the last time she had been out for dinner. She at last agreed and Hamish had to wait until she took an old fur coat out of its wrappings so that she would be "suitably" dressed.

Hamish went outside to wait for her. His boot caught the saucer of milk outside the door and tipped it over. He phoned Malcolm Douglas, who agreed to try to make pictures of Annie's visitors. Hamish warned him not to laugh at any mention of fairies.

Annie came out and locked the door behind her. She saw the spilled milk and let out an exclamation of dismay. "It's a bad omen," she cried. "They've never rejected my milk afore."

Hamish somehow did not want to admit having knocked the milk over. "Probably the wind," he said. "Let's get going."

In Lochinver, at Malcolm's studio, Annie turned out to be a good witness, for Peter Gaunt's appearance was burnt into her brain. Hamish surveyed the drawing with satisfaction. Now, he thought, for the difficult bit.

"The wee man who came for the gunman. Can you describe him?" he asked.

"I do not think that would be right," she said primly.

"They do the best duck breast at The Caberfeidh," crooned Hamish. "Melts in your mouth, it does."

Annie's diet before the recent windfall had been food in discounted bashed tins.

She thought of the spilled milk. It was a sign that they would come for her. Nothing mattered now.

She gave an accurate description. Hamish studied the result. He thought the fairy could be Mexican or even North African.

He then took Annie out for dinner, hoping he could put the meal down on expenses.

Annie ate heartily but regaled Hamish again with all her miseries. "I'll call on you tomorrow and get you to make a signed statement."

"I will not be there."

"Where will you be?"

"The fairies will have taken me. I must pay my debt."

People talk about someone being away with the fairies, thought Hamish angrily, but this is ridiculous. He persuaded the restaurant to let him use their computer and printer. He hastily typed out a statement, ran off three copies, and got Annie to sign them.

He was relieved when he dropped her off. Still, he thought as he drove away, people up here living in areas not even as remote as Annie's start to go round the bend.

She decided to write her will. She had little to leave, just a couple of thousand. Annie thought hard. She had no one to leave the money to.

At last, she left her cottage, money, and belongings to Sergeant Hamish Macbeth of Lochdubh with the request that he build a granite monument to the fairies outside the cottage.

She then walked to her neighbours and got them to sign her will.

Annie was panting by the time she got home, and a pain was shooting down her arm. She had just got over the threshold when she suffered a massive heart attack and died.

Hamish had driven straight to headquarters in Strathbane. He left the sketches and statements for Jimmy before making his weary way back to Lochdubh.

He was roused early in the morning by Jimmy. "Get back to that auld woman," said Jimmy, "and see what more you can get out of her. Police Scotland are fed up with us. They are getting together a special team to take over the investigation. Blair is screaming it's not necessary but word has gone down from that new police commissioner that we're not getting anywhere."

Hamish took his time getting to Annie's cottage. It was a rare fine day, one of those days in the north when, even in winter, a balmy breeze blew in from the Gulf Stream and the sky above the mountains was pale blue.

He stopped on the way there, let the dog and cat out to play, unwrapped a breakfast consisting of a bacon bap, and opened up a flask of coffee. Hamish thought wryly that if Dick had still been with him, a table would have been set and Dick would have been frying up a full breakfast on his camping stove.

When he was finished, he reluctantly whistled for Sonsie and Lugs, put them into the back of the Land Rover again. He felt guilty at not having told Annie that it had been he who had knocked over that saucer of milk. Odd that this belief in fairies should persist. Some thought of them as tiny creatures, dressed in green; others like Annie believed they were more like elves.

The first thing he saw with a sinking heart was Annie's two brogued feet sticking out of her open front door. He stopped the Land Rover and ran to her. There was no pulse, and her face was twisted in a death rictus of agony.

Hamish felt a superstitious shudder go through him. Black clouds were racing in from the west, and a rising wind keened in the heather.

He phoned for an ambulance and then phoned police headquarters to report a death that might be suspicious. He dared not go further into the house for fear of disturbing what might turn out to be a crime scene.

Hamish reflected later that he had never seen so many people at a death scene. A helicopter was the first to arrive with Daviot and a tall, thin grey man with a great beak of a nose overshadowing a small mouth.

"Sergeant Macbeth," said Daviot in a cold voice, "this is Detective Chief Superintendent Ross Douglas."

"Begin at the beginning," said Douglas.

Hamish told him about Annie's adventures and how he had to take a statement from her at the restaurant because she was sure the fairies would come for her during the night. Cars and vans screeched to a halt as the full force of the law arrived.

Jimmy joined them, ushering forward a thickset man. "This is Miss MacDougal's neighbour. He said that Annie called on him late last night so that he and his wife could witness her will."

"Your name?" demanded Douglas.

"Ulysses MacSporran."

Douglas went up in Hamish's estimation. Blair would have jeered at the name.

"And, Mr. MacSporran, who benefits?"

"A police sergeant called Hamish Macbeth."

Douglas turned cold eyes on Hamish. "Did you know of this?"

"No, I did not, sir. If there are any living relatives, they are welcome to contest that will. She was a wee bit off her head with this fairy business. She said she was going to die during the night."

"Did she fear the men would come back? In that case, Sergeant, you should not have left her alone."

Patiently Hamish explained about the spilled milk and said that Annie thought the fairies would come for her.

"Strange," commented Douglas. "We will await the results of the autopsy. In the meantime, Macbeth, you are suspended from duty. If it turns out to be murder, we might think you did it, knowing she was going to leave everything to you."

"But, sir…"

"Off with you. And wait in your police station for further instructions."

Hamish spent the next three days anxiously waiting. Normally, he would have called at the hotel to see Priscilla, but he was too worried. He dusted and cleaned the police station, attended to his sheep and hens, and then took his rod up to the River Anstey to see if he could poach a salmon.

He caught four trout instead and was just about to go into the station when he heard himself being hailed. He turned round. The tall figure of Douglas was just getting out of the back of a car.

"Sir?"

"Inside, Macbeth."

Hamish went into the kitchen, followed by his dog and cat.

Douglas sat down wearily at the kitchen table. "You will be glad to know that Miss MacDougal died of a massive heart attack. According to the procurator fiscal, it could have happened at any time."

Douglas had an almost accentless voice with faint Glaswegian undertones.

"It was right good of ye to call in person to tell me, sir," said Hamish. "Would you like a dram?"

"Why not? My driver can wait."

Hamish took down a bottle and two glasses. "The neighbours and local people report that Mrs. MacDougal, as far as they know, had no living relatives. Do you want to pay for the funeral?"

"Of course," said Hamish. "Did she say what kind of funeral she wanted?"

"She wanted to be cremated."

"When the body is released, I'll arrange it," said Hamish.

"And will you build that monument to the fairies?"

"I suppose I am honour-bound to do so."

Douglas eyed the dog and cat, who were now sleeping by the stove.

"Is that a wild cat?"

"No," said Hamish sharply. Wild cats were so rare in Scotland that he always feared Sonsie would be taken away from him. "It iss chust a verra big cat."

The sibilance of Hamish's accent showed he was nervous.

Douglas sipped his whisky and looked around at all the gleaming appliances in the kitchen, from the espresso machine to the dishwasher.

"You do well for yourself here," he commented.

"Only for a short period now, sir," said Hamish. "Dick Fraser won all these gadgets on television quizzes. He is leaving the force to set up as a baker and he will be soon taking all this with him."

"I am amazed that there is still a police station here," said the superintendent.

"It is because nothing in policing beats a man on the ground. If not me, who would check on the old people? Sutherland is vast, and many people are isolated."

"I have been checking up on you." Douglas looked at Hamish curiously. "Surely a bright man like you would want some advancement?"

"I consider the quality of life more important than any advancement, sir."

"You are a maverick, and I don't like mavericks. A good police force is like the army. I like men who obey orders and I like ambitious men."

"Meaning you don't like me."

"I feel that remark is impertinent."

Hamish sighed. "If I may say so, sir, this could be valuable time spent discussing the case, rather than my character. I have fresh trout just caught. Perhaps you would like to stay for dinner?"

There was a long silence. The fire crackled in the stove.

Douglas rose to his feet. "I'll tell my driver to come back in an hour and a half."

*   *   *

As he fried the trout dipped in oatmeal and boiled potatoes, Hamish told the superintendent about Heather Green. "I wished I could have taken some of that money and given it to her."

"Peter Gaunt is an evil man. We've had more reports about him. He is also wanted by the Florida police for fraud. But all his criminal activities have been conning money out of vulnerable people. We have not made public the finding of the money, and we are keeping watch on the church in case he comes back for it."

Hamish opened a bottle of wine. "The murders, the tortures. I feel there is even bigger money involved. It's my belief that the Southerns were used to get something valuable out of Canada. They did not go where they were meant to go but tried to disappear in the Highlands. But how Liz Bentley comes into this, I do not know. There is no record of her having given money to Gaunt, although she attended his church."

He suddenly stopped talking and gazed vacantly at the superintendent. Then he said, "I've missed something important."

"And what is that?"

"Thon church was by way of being a social club, dances and all. In these days of digital cameras and mobile phones, I bet there are photos around. I would like to see if there is some evidence of some man or other besides Gaunt romancing Liz."

Douglas rose to his feet. "I'll get on to it right away. Why did no one think of this before?"

"Why didn't I?" said Hamish, furious with himself.

"That was a grand supper. Thank you."

"Sir, when you collect photos, may I see them?"

"Yes, I will let you know."

In the next few days, Blair, who was smarting over being excluded from the special investigative team, learned that this superintendent was crediting none other than Hamish Macbeth with the idea of collecting the photographs. Racked with spite and jealousy, he waited until the superintendent was leaving police headquarters and waylaid him.

"Sir, a word in your ear."

"And you are?"

"Chief Detective Inspector Blair."

"So what information do you have, Blair?"

"I just wanted tae warn ye about Macbeth."

"Why?"

"He disnae obey orders and he's not quite right in the head, if you ask me."

Douglas looked down at Blair, noticing the ravages of drink on his swollen face.

"There is no shame these days, Blair," he said

evenly, "in admitting to being an alcoholic. There are excellent rehabs around. I suggest you check into one."

He turned and strode off.

In that moment, Blair could have killed Hamish Macbeth. It was Macbeth that was responsible for all his humiliations. It must have been Macbeth who had told Douglas that he, Blair, was an alcoholic. This time it was open war. He'd get that damn highlander off the force if it was the last thing he could do.

The sketches of Peter Gaunt and the "fairy" appeared in all the newspapers and television channels. Then Hamish was summoned to Strathbane by Douglas to look over a selection of photographs.

To Blair's fury, he learned that the conference room was to be allocated to Hamish. The photographs were spread out on the long table there.

Hamish had left the dog and cat behind as they could get in and out through the large flap on the door. He had asked Angela to look after them, but she had refused. She said they terrified her cats. Hamish guessed both pets would head along to the Italian restaurant and mooch for food at the kitchen door. He was worried about them getting overweight.

He gloomily surveyed the photographs. If this were television, he thought, they would be flashed up onto a screen and I would be saying, *Hold it right there. Zoom in on that one.*

He sat down and scrutinised photographs of beetle drives, sales of work, dances, and outings. Liz was in several of them. Often she was photographed standing close to Peter Gaunt. In one shot of the church, the statue loomed over the congregation. He peered at it. The things he hadn't thought of! Where had that giant statue come from? Who had made it?

He phoned Jimmy and asked him if they had any idea who had made the statue.

"We checked that," said Jimmy. "Ordered from a website, churcheffigies.com. They must have altered it when they got it."

Hamish thanked him and went back to his work. At last, he focussed on one of the larger photographs. It was of a picnic on the banks of Loch Ness. It was a group photograph. He took out a magnifying glass and scanned the faces. There was Liz Bentley. The man behind her was largely obscured by a taller man in front. Hamish could only make out the side of the man's face. He could swear it was tattooed. Was this the tattooed man who had taken Peter Gaunt away?

He diligently searched through the other photographs. He was despairing of ever finding that elusive man again when suddenly there he was. It was a shot of dancers performing the Dashing White Sergeant; through a gap in the dancers, he could see Liz talking earnestly to a small man with tattoos on his face. He was holding her hand.

He seized the photo and ran downstairs, nearly colliding with Superintendent Douglas, who was coming up accompanied by a group of detectives.

Douglas stopped. "Anything, Macbeth?"

Hamish showed him the photograph. "I'm off to the supermarket to interview two girls who attended the church to show them this. It's the connection I've been looking for."

"Take Anderson. You'll find him at his desk."

While Jimmy and Hamish waited for the arrival of Beryl and Ellie in the supermarket manager's office, which he had allowed them to use for the interview, Jimmy said, "I wonder why they didn't kill Annie MacDougal. I mean, you'd never have got that sketch otherwise."

"Maybe he's just a sidekick and not a killer," said Hamish.

The door opened and the girls walked in. Hamish pulled out chairs for them and then handed them the photograph, pointing to the tattooed man. "Do you know him?" he asked.

Ellie gave a nervous giggle. "He's the one folk got their drugs from. Scary wee man. Liz was all over him. But she was aye all over anything in trousers that showed a bit o' interest in her."

Beryl said, "He was only around for a month. Then the police came round one night to look for drugs. They couldn't find anything and the wee man had disappeared. He had a funny sort of accent."

"Can you take a guess?"

But all they would say was that it was sort of foreign, but they didn't know which foreign.

They could not add anything more of interest, but Hamish felt elated. Slowly and surely, the threads of investigation were being drawn together.

Chapter Nine

☠

"That's the reason they're called lessons," the Gryphon re-marked: "because they lessen from day to day."

—*Lewis Carroll*

But suddenly, the case just died. Detectives hidden outside the church waited and waited but no one came. Winter slowly released its grip on the Highlands.

Hamish dealt with petty crimes and sheep dip papers. Priscilla had left a long time ago. The Frenchman had left shortly afterwards. Hamish often wondered if he had followed her to London, where Priscilla worked as a computer expert for a bank in the City.

He occasionally visited Ellie and Beryl again in the hope that they could remember something they might have forgotten, but without success.

He had commissioned a monument to the fairies to be built and had had a copper plaque inserted on it, saying IN MEMORY OF ANNIE MACDOUGAL, TAKEN BY

THE FAIRIES. He had put the house up for sale, but he was not expecting to find a buyer for such a remote croft house with no land attached.

To his delight, it was bought as a holiday home by a pair of aged hippies who believed in fairies. Hamish transferred the money from the sale to his family in Rogart. His overjoyed mother had promptly begun arrangements to take the whole family—her husband and Hamish's two small brothers—on a cruise.

If, he calculated, the villains had decided all that money was not worth collecting, then it stood to reason they were after something greater.

He often wondered, also, about the odd partnership of Anka and Dick. They had established their bakery in Braikie and it was a great success. They had been written up in several newspapers and had even appeared on Grampian television. Hamish had tried to ask Anka out on a date but she had only smiled—while Dick had glared—and said she was too busy.

He then had taken Christine, the forensic expert, out for dinner. But the failure of the investigation hung over them, and the date was not successful for either of them.

Usually he would have been happy with his quiet life, but he could not settle down. Surely some clue to the mystery could be found.

April arrived with the usual depressing "lambing blizzard," briefly turning the countryside white again.

But after a few days, balmy breezes blew in from the Gulf Stream.

Superintendent Douglas had never contacted Hamish again, and he learned from Jimmy that the special team had moved their headquarters to Glasgow.

He suddenly decided to visit that church again. He had found the money when no one else had.

The police tape was gone and the church crouched in the evening gloaming beside the dark waters of Loch Ness. So far, the recent police watch had saved the building from vandals. The door was securely padlocked; it took Hamish almost three-quarters of an hour to pick the lock.

The statue had been taken away. The finding of the money had been broadcast at last, causing a sensation in the newspapers which soon died away. Hamish began a search, feeling under the pews and the altar, hunting through the side rooms and kitchen.

Suddenly he stiffened. The church was suffused in an eerie blue light. He ran to the window and looked out. A television van was parked outside and Elspeth Grant was making a speech to camera. He felt a surge of gladness, all the old attraction she held for him rushing back.

He waited until she had finished and the lights were switched off and made his way outside.

"Hamish!" cried Elspeth. "Is there anything new?"

He shook his head. "What brings you here?"

"We're doing a documentary on the unsolved murders. Real crime features are all the rage and they hope to sell this to America. Can you make a statement?"

"Can't," said Hamish gloomily. "I'd need to ask for permission and, believe me, I wouldnae get it. Where are you staying?"

"We've made the Tommel Castle Hotel our headquarters."

Hamish smiled down at her, remembering the Elspeth of old when she was working on the local paper, an Elspeth with frizzy hair and thrift shop clothes. All that remained of the old Elspeth in the sophisticated figure before him were those silvery-grey Gypsy eyes.

His strengthening accent betrayed his sudden nervousness. "Is there any chance of us getting together for chust a wee talk?" he asked.

"All right. We've got what we need here. We're just about to head back to the hotel. Join me for dinner."

Hamish raced back to the police station to change into his one good suit. Sonsie and Lugs eyed him gloomily, knowing that the suit usually meant they were to be left behind. Apart from his pleasure at meeting Elspeth again, Hamish longed to discuss the case with her. In the past, Elspeth's strange psychic abilities had hit on things he had overlooked.

He hoped Priscilla was not at the hotel, knowing

that Elspeth blamed her for the breakup of their engagement. When she had seen him on film in a previous case spending time with Priscilla, it caused her to get drunk and behave so outrageously with another man that it had been reported in the newspapers.

He hoped he would not have to share a table with Elspeth's crew, but when he arrived in the dining room he found that Elspeth had secured a small table for both of them in a corner.

He kissed her on the cheek. She smelled of expensive French perfume. He suddenly remembered the days when the old Elspeth smelled of heather and peat smoke.

"The new me is here to stay," said Elspeth. "Get used to it."

"I hate the way you can sometimes read my mind," said Hamish.

Elspeth studied the menu. "I'm going to start with a shrimp cocktail," she said. "I always liked them, and they've come back into fashion."

"Never knew they went out," commented Hamish. "I'll have the venison pâté."

"And they've got roast rabbit," said Elspeth. "That's very fashionable now."

"I hate it when cheap food becomes fashionable," said Hamish. "The price goes up. I'll have the fillet steak."

When they ordered their meals and a bottle of Merlot,

Elspeth began to talk about her life at the television station in Glasgow, and then broke off and looked at Hamish with amusement. "You aren't listening. You want to talk murder. Well, you can wait for the coffee."

So Hamish politely waited. Then when the coffee arrived, he began to tell her everything he knew. Around them, the diners gradually left, and when he had finished, they were alone in the dining room.

"What do you think?" he asked eagerly.

"I agree with you that I think there's something worth much more than the stuff in the statue," said Elspeth. "There's slavery. Bring in illegal immigrants and sell them to the gang bosses who make them work for nothing."

"That's usually where there's lots of agriculture," Hamish pointed out. "Nothing really up here but sheep."

"Prostitution?"

"I thought of that, but whoever tortured the Southerns and Liz were looking for something hidden. Hard to hide a load of women brought in and forced into prostitution. I think it must be drugs. It all started in Canada. An awful lot of Ecstasy is manufactured in Canada. But maybe cocaine. Say a load arrived from somewhere like Colombia and they wanted to take it over to Britain. It's awfy hard to police all the bays and inlets on the coast. It comes in a large ship and then is transferred to a small boat which can creep in and avoid the customs people. Now, I think the Southerns might have been a couple of wasters who knew Peter Gaunt. Maybe they've been to Sutherland before. So they tell whoever about a safe way of getting the drugs into Britain. Gaunt introduces them to the head villain. The Southerns agree to hide the drugs. But they make up their minds to put them somewhere no one would think of until any search for them dies down. I think Gaunt knows where the stuff is, but Gaunt is on the run, possibly not only from the police but also from the boss of the whole operation."

"So why did he take so long to disappear?" asked Elspeth. "I mean, you would think in that case that he would have fled after the murders."

"He could...what is it, Clarry?" he asked as the chef came up to their table.

"Just some bones for Lugs and a bit o' fish for Sonsie. How are you, Miss Grant?"

"I'm fine. How are you and the family?"

Hamish fretted until Clarry had left. "He could have persuaded whoever that he had been tricked just like them. I mean, when he fled, we assumed it was because we were closing in on him for fraud. But what if they decided he really did know something. He could be lying dead somewhere."

"If they tortured him, wouldn't he talk?"

"Yes, he would," agreed Hamish. "And if that is the case, they've got the goods and are long gone."

"But why didn't the fake Leighs, the Southerns, tell them?"

"Maybe they passed the goods over to Gaunt. He promised them their cut for handling the operation but did not tell them where he had stashed the stuff."

"As you have nothing else to go on," said Elspeth, "maybe you should be looking for Gaunt's dead body. There might be some forensic clues there." She stifled a yawn.

"I've kept you up late," said Hamish. "I'll get the bill."

"Don't worry, I'll get it," said Elspeth. "It'll go on my expenses." She called for the waiter and paid the bill. "Where will you start your search?"

"Maybe up near where Annie had her cottage. There are shepherd's bothies up on the hills, abandoned crofts, places like that. What will you do now?"

"I've got enough background. Back to Glasgow tomorrow."

He looked at her sadly. "And is that it?"

Elspeth gathered up her belongings and said curtly, "Don't go there again. I'm tired. Good night."

And before Hamish could rise from his chair, she had sped out of the dining room.

The following morning, Hamish packed up the Land Rover with the dog and cat, a picnic, a stove, and a tent. It was a fine sunny day. As he drove north, he cursed the monsters who had brought their blackness to this beautiful wild part of the world: a place of huge mountains, white beaches, and tiny villages where the people still spoke with the finest accent in the British Isles, although a sort of bastardised Glaswegian was creeping into Inverness.

He diligently searched abandoned ruins and bothies, questioning crofters as to whether they had seen strangers in the area. He had only stopped for lunch, and by the end of the day he was tired. He went to Cromish and bought eggs, sausages, and bacon, and food for Sonsie and Lugs.

He found a camping place on a deserted beach, put up his tent, lit the camping stove, and fried up the sausages, bacon, and egg.

As he fell asleep to the sound of the waves, with the cat beside him and the dog at his feet, he decided to search only one more day. He was not to know that Peter Gaunt would be found the following day, closer to home.

Rod Monteith was a lowland Scot whose home was in Dumfries. He was the owner of fifty stationery shops in the south of Scotland and the north of England. He had remained a bachelor until his early forties. His faithful elderly secretary, Mrs. Struther, had died, leaving him to find a replacement. During the interviews, he met Amanda Burke. She was highly unsuitable, having none of the secretarial skills she claimed to have. But she was dainty and blonde, and had an exquisite figure. Dazzled by a woman for the first time in his life, Rod took her out for dinner instead, embarked on a whirlwind romance, and proposed marriage.

After a year of marriage, Amanda, who had seen an old film about Bonnie Prince Charlie, said she yearned for a holiday cottage in the Highlands. Rod was already tiring of his empty-headed wife, but he thought perhaps if he bought somewhere in the north, then Amanda might spend time up there and leave him occasionally on his own, for the only time he could find relief from her endless prattle was when she was seated in front of the television.

So he had bought a square Victorian building on the edge of Cnothan. At first Amanda was delighted with her new "toy," and as she set about refurbishing the house, he found he could stay in the south and leave her to it.

But Cnothan was a sour, unfriendly place. Amanda's romance with the Highlands began to pall. She phoned her husband and said she wanted to sell the place. Rod told her to put it on the market but she screeched that was man's work and he should travel to Cnothan immediately.

Rod now had an efficient secretary, a tall angular woman in her forties with lank hair and thick glasses.

He found her intelligent and restful. Amanda was in her twenties and as restful as a bed of nails.

He arrived in Cnothan. The sturdy Victorian walls of the villa stared down at Amanda's frilly furnishings and pink walls.

She greeted him flinging her arms around him and bursting into tears. She had a strong grip despite her outwards appearance of frailty, and he had a feeling he was being trapped in the coils of some reptile. When she had recovered, she said the old outside privy in the garden must be removed.

"Maybe it will add to the old charm of the place," said Rod.

"Charm? Come with me. It's disgusting," said Amanda.

He followed her out into the garden, reflecting that only Amanda would think of wearing stilettos in the Highlands as she performed a sort of slalom between the plastic gnomes.

She unlatched the door and flung it open and then screamed and screamed, before collapsing and striking her neck on the sharp broken top of the pointed hat of one of the gnomes.

In the privy, dumped on the old wooden seat of the toilet, was a dead man. From the smell, it seemed as if he had been dead for some time. A cloud of blackflies rose from his body.

Rod ran into the house to call the police. He didn't bother about his wife. Amanda, he knew, from bitter experience, enjoyed faking faints. He phoned the police and sat down and waited. In his upset, he forgot to go and check on his wife.

When Jimmy Anderson and the whole investigative circus arrived, Rod was lucky it was Jimmy and not Blair. For his wife was found to be dead, and Blair would no doubt have arrested him on the spot.

Hamish got the message and raced back all the way to Cnothan. Christine and her team had just finished their work, and Jimmy was ready to go and examine the privy for himself when Hamish joined him.

He said a preliminary examination had shown that Amanda had fallen and the cap of the gnome had pierced her neck.

"So who's the dead man?" asked Hamish.

"Let's have a look." Jimmy led the way to the privy.

Hamish held a handkerchief up to his nose. "It looks like Peter Gaunt. Anything in the pockets?"

"Nothing."

"Did the pathologist say whether there were signs of torture?"

"Won't know until he does a thorough examination. You'd better go off and knock on doors."

"You've got police all over the village. I saw them going from house to house when I drove through."

"You know what Cnothan is like. They hate talking to outsiders. They might talk to you."

"Can I have a wee word with the husband first?"

"Oh, go on. I hope his wife's death was really accidental, because he doesn't exactly seem moved."

Rod was sitting on a frilly pink couch in the living room. Hamish thought it was the first time he had actually seen a frilly couch. It was covered in slippery rose-pink silk. There were frills down the seams and frills at floor level. Rod's face stood out white against the background.

Hamish introduced himself. "It's the shock," said Rod. "Poor Amanda. She was always saying how delicate she was and that her heart was not good. God forgive me. I didn't believe her."

"Why was that?" asked Hamish. Rod was a tall slim man, impeccably dressed in a well-tailored suit. He had grey hair and a grey lugubrious face with a thin mouth and large grey eyes.

"Amanda was always claiming to be delicate. She always seemed to be acting a part. I think the shock has killed her apart from that blow to the head."

"When did you arrive?"

"Today. Am I a suspect? My secretary and staff will tell you that I was there until yesterday evening. I set off right away and then stopped overnight in Perth before coming on up here." He went on to tell Hamish about his wife's recently exploded romantic ideas about the Highlands.

They would check that gnome for fingerprints,

thought Hamish, in case Rod had seen an opportunity and brained his wife. But diligent questioning could produce nothing useful.

People sometimes compared villages like Cnothan, slap bang in the middle of nowhere, to Welsh villages at the end of valleys. Strangers were regarded as people from a few miles away, and the motto of Cnothan should have been, "We keep ourselves to ourselves."

As he watched police going from door to door, Hamish reflected that he would only be covering old ground.

He still had food in the Land Rover, so, along with his pets, he drove up on the moors, well away from the village, and parked. He was hungry again, so he fried himself up some sausages after having fed Sonsie and Lugs and then stretched out on the grass and stared vacantly at the sky.

He drifted off to sleep and woke half an hour later with his phone ringing.

It was Jimmy. "Got anything?" he asked.

"Nothing," said Hamish.

"There's another extensive manhunt for Gaunt's tattooed companion."

"How's the husband doing?"

"He is being berated by Blair, who turned up not so long ago. Fortunately for the man, Daviot arrived in time to stop Blair charging Mr. Monteith with murder.

I don't think we can do much else until the autopsies. Look, Hamish. I need one of your flashes of highland intuition. Get back to your station and go over all the reports and statements and see if you can think of one thing."

Hamish agreed, and rang off.

The police station seemed a bit bleak without Dick. He went to make himself a cup of coffee and then realised the espresso machine was missing. It was then he saw a note addressed to himself on the kitchen table.

"Dear Hamish," he read. "I called last night but you were out. I've collected a few of my things. Do come and see us soon. Yours aye, Dick."

Hamish went through to the living room. The large flat-screen television had gone, along with the recorder and all the stereo equipment.

He went back to the kitchen. The dishwasher had been taken away as well. Hamish could only be glad that Dick had left the washing machine. But he had taken the electric kettle. Hamish lit the stove and put the kettle on top and waited for it to boil.

The kitchen door opened and Angela Brodie walked in. "I brought you a cake," she said. "It's a new recipe. Ginger."

"That's very kind of you, Angela. The kettle will soon be boiling. Would you like a cup of coffee?"

"Where's that espresso gadget?"

"Dick's taken it to his new quarters."

"Will he and Anka get married?" asked Angela.

"Dinnae be daft. She's a goddess and he's a wee round man."

"A lot of women would fancy Dick. He's, well, comfy."

Hamish looked at her uneasily. He still had dreams of getting the beautiful Anka out on a date.

"I dinnae know women went for comfy."

"Comfy and a homemaker and a champion baker. It's quite a lot, Hamish."

"Can't see it. Sit down and I'll get your coffee."

"The phone's been ringing all morning," said Angela. "Folk are saying there's two dead bodies over at Cnothan."

"Aye, that's right." Hamish made instant coffee and told her about it.

"Cnothan will soon be swamped with the press," said Angela.

"Well, good luck to the poor sods. They won't get a single quote."

"Oh, yes they will," said Angela cynically. "They'll say to someone, 'You must all be very frightened,' to which the person may reply, 'Aye,' before slamming the door. So in the paper next morning you will read, 'Pale and trembling, Mrs. Blank Blank said, "We are all frightened."'"

Hamish stared at her. "You've given me an idea."

"Have some of my cake and tell me."

Hamish reluctantly cut a slice, for Angela was as famous for her lousy baking as Anka and Dick were famous for their baps and cakes.

A brown sticky liquid oozed out of the cake. "Oh, dear," said Angela. "Mrs. Wellington gave me that recipe and said it was foolproof."

"Never mind," said Hamish, opening a tin. "Have a bit o' shortbread instead."

"So what's your idea?" asked Angela.

"You could start gossiping for me. Say Hamish Macbeth knows what it is the villains want and he knows where it is hidden."

"They'll kill you! You're going to put yourself up as bait."

"I'll be on the alert. Please, Angela."

"All right," she said reluctantly. "But what if this gossip gets back to headquarters?"

"Won't matter. I'll deny the whole thing."

"Then so will I," said Angela.

Chapter Ten

Let us do—or die!

—*Robert Burns*

Angela busily gossiped, telling each person about Hamish knowing where the mysterious loot was hidden and swearing each one to secrecy.

The Currie sisters were wide-eyed. "Why doesn't he produce it?" asked Nessie.

"Produce it?" echoed her sister.

"He hopes they'll come for it and that way he will trap them," said Angela.

And so the news crept out from Lochdubh to the surrounding countryside.

When the news reached Dick, he said to Anka, "I think he's hoping the murderers will come after him and that way he'll find out who they are. I feel I should be down there, looking after him."

"He's got the whole of the Scottish police force behind him," said Anka.

"Maybe he hasnae told them."

"Why would he do a stupid thing like that?"

"Because he's Hamish."

After two weeks had passed, Hamish began to fear that nothing would happen. The autopsies on the bodies of Amanda Monteith and Peter Gaunt had proved that Gaunt had died of a massive heart attack, perhaps brought on by fear, and that the blow to Amanda's head was not the cause of her death, but that she, too, had suffered a heart attack.

Hamish decided to go down to Inverness and do some shopping. He could have bought everything he wanted in Patel's shop, but he suddenly wanted to get away from the village.

The miracle of Inverness was that it kept expanding without anyone quite knowing where all the money to create its boom had come from. Hamish's mother had said the old people remembered Inverness when it was a sleepy little town where the highland cattle were driven down the main street from the stockyards at the railway station. It had been full then of privately owned little shops. Now every giant supermarket seemed to have moved in.

It was a fine day. He had shopped for picnic supplies for his animals, a new sweater and socks, and was heading for the car park when he saw Scully Baird in front of him.

Hamish caught up with him. "How's it going, Scully? You look well."

Scully had put on weight, and there was colour in his cheeks. "I've got a job," he said proudly.

"Let's go for a coffee," said Hamish, "and tell me about it."

They turned into a coffee shop which had a bewildering array of types of coffee on order. Hamish ordered an Americano and Scully, a latte.

"So tell me all about it," said Hamish.

"I'd nearly given up hope at the job centre wi' all the Poles snatching up every job," said Scully, "but I finally got one. It's at the crematorium."

"What do you do there? Burn the bodies?"

"No, I've got a cosy little number. I sort out the ashes into cardboard boxes."

"I thought they all went into urns," said Hamish.

"Naw. Some folk want them scattered and, would you believe it, some mean sods never turn up to collect the dear departed."

"So what happens to the ashes?"

"Trade secret. It's ma day off. I get a day off during the week if I've been working at the weekend. Tell you what. I'm right proud of my wee office. When we finish, come back with me and see it."

"I don't want to leave Sonsie and Lugs in the car too long."

"Bring them with you," said Scully. "They can have a wee run outside the crematorium."

"All right. I'll run you there," said Hamish.

*   *   *

At the crematorium in Strathbane, Hamish let the dog and cat out of the Land Rover and followed Scully to his little office.

"I've got my ain desk, see?" said Scully proudly.

"Are the Wrights good bosses?"

"Aye, they're grand. I hope they don't become my customers, though."

"Why is that?"

"I think they've both got Parkinson's. They shake a lot, spill their coffee. I walked into Mr. Kenneth's office and forgot to knock, and he turned white and clutched his heart."

Hamish looked sharply at Scully. "Didn't you think they might be frightened of something?"

"What of?" Scully laughed. "Ghosts? Come on, man. They've been dealing with the dead for years. Got tae pee. Back in a mo."

Scully had left his keys on the desk. Hamish fished in his capacious pocket and pulled out a square of wax. He carefully took impressions of the keys and then hurriedly replaced them when he heard Scully returning.

"You've done well for yourself," said Hamish, reflecting that not many people would think of it as a great job, but Scully had changed so much from the drug-wrecked youth he once had been.

*   *   *

Hamish drove out of Strathbane and stopped up on the moors to feed himself and his pets. It had been an impulse to take impressions of Scully's keys: an impulse prompted by Scully thinking the Wright brothers had Parkinson's. Hamish wondered if their shakes were caused by fear. There had been some tenuous tie between Gaunt and the crematorium.

He looked around the sunny countryside. If only things could go back to normal. The unsolved murders seemed to send a blackness creeping over the landscape.

Hamish wondered whether to pay a visit to the seer, Angus Macdonald. He had often suspected that Angus was taking money from the gullible, claiming to be able to get in touch with their dead loved ones, but so far had not been able to find any proof. He packed up the remains of the picnic, whistled for Sonsie and Lugs, and went back to Lochdubh, where he left them at the police station.

Angus always expected a gift. Hamish went to the cupboard in Dick's old room, knowing that that was where Dick stored a lot of the smaller prizes he had won in pub quizzes. Dick had left most of the stuff. Hamish found a pretty little imitation carriage clock. That would do.

As he walked up the brae to Angus's cottage, he

suddenly had a feeling of being watched. But when he turned round, a glaring red setting sun was in his eyes.

Angus was standing by the open door, waiting for him. He accepted the carriage clock and put it carefully on the mantelpiece over the fireplace.

When they were seated in Angus's living room, Hamish asked, "What do you know of Kenneth and Robert Wright?"

"The funeral directors?"

"Aye, them."

"Had a bad time a whiles back," said Angus. "There's Scott, the rival funeral people, but the Wrights have the crematorium. But then there came this visiting minister, telling folk that it was a sin to get their loved ones cremated, for how were they to rise whole on the Day of Judgement? Hellfire was for the burning of folk. Trade fell right off and it looked as if they would have to sell up. But they got money from somewhere, people got over that nonsense, and soon they were doing well again."

"Any idea where they got the money from?"

"No."

"I think they are afraid," said Hamish.

"If they got money from a loan shark and are having a hard time paying it off, they've got every reason to be afraid."

"No psychic abilities working today, Angus?"

"A wee clock won by Mr. Fraser might be considered a bit cheap by the spirits."

"You're a waste o' space," said Hamish, getting to his feet.

"And you're a tethered goat, laddie."

"What?"

"You dinnae know where the loot is. You just put that about in the hope they'll come for you." Angus half closed his eyes. "Aye, and they will. They could be at the foot o' the brae right now. Take these pets o' yours and give them to Dick Fraser to look after. Anyone after you would want rid o' them first."

Hamish gave him a startled look. He left hurriedly and ran all the way to the police station. He loaded Sonsie and Lugs into the Land Rover and raced to Braikie.

The shop front was closed but there were lights on in the bakery at the back. Hamish went round and knocked at the door.

Dick opened the door and smiled in delight as he bent down to pat the animals. He was wearing a white coat and a white skullcap.

"Come in. Sit yourself down. I'll get you a coffee."

The tall figure of Anka said, "No animals in the bakery."

"These are hygienic animals," said Dick.

Anka shrugged and went on kneading dough.

Hamish told Dick about his worries. "I'll take them upstairs now," said Dick. "We've got a flat up there."

Hamish followed him up. The flat above was spacious although very low-ceilinged. "They'll be fine here," said Dick. "Leave them for as long as you like. I've missed them."

Lugs wagged his plume of a tail and Sonsie let out a low purr.

"Won't Anka object?" asked Hamish.

"No. She won't want them around in the shop or the bakery, but they can stay here."

"But you will exercise them?"

"I've got time off during the day. We've a couple o' lassies serving in the shop."

"How are you getting on with Anka?"

"Just grand. We're pals."

How can you just be pals with a Venus like that? was what Hamish wanted to say. Instead he asked, "Do you think Anka might come out for dinner with me one night?"

Dick was petting Sonsie's fur. His hand tightened on her coat, and she gave out a low hiss of warning.

"Why don't you ask her?" said Dick.

"I'll be off then," said Hamish. "I'll talk to Anka on the way out."

Dick crept to the top of the stairs and listened. He heard Hamish say, "If you're free one evening, would you like to have dinner with me?"

"With Dick as well?"

"Well, I thought, just us."

She slid a tray of scones into the oven and said over her shoulder, "I don't like to go anywhere without Dick."

"In that case, we'll all have dinner together."

"Ask Dick about it."

"I shall next time I call."

Dick retreated into the flat. He hugged the cat and then the dog. "There is a God," he said.

Hamish drove slowly back to Lochdubh, feeling sulky. Here he was, putting his life on the line while Dick Fraser had not only Anka as company but now his pets as well.

The realisation that he was bitterly jealous of Dick made him feel ashamed of himself. "Why am I always chasing dreams?" he demanded the walls of the police station. "Why am I always chasing after impossible women?" His thoughts turned to Christine Dalray, the forensic expert. He would ask her out. She was keen on him, he knew that.

But the following day found him heading back to Cromish. Dr. Williams had phoned him early in the morning, saying, "You'd better get up here fast before there's another murder."

It transpired that an incomer had bought Liz Bentley's cottage. She had moved from Edinburgh. Her name was Samantha Trent, "call me Sam," and at first she had seemed harmless enough, going round the village, yakking on about the quality of life, which was the acidulous way the doctor had put it. But to the horror of the villagers, she was guilty of a heinous crime. She was seen feeding a fox. "So you see," the doctor has said, "folk are so riled up, they might shoot her."

Townies and their mad love affair wi' sodding foxes, thought Hamish.

He parked outside Liz's cottage and rang the bell. The door was answered by a tall woman, wearing an army sweater, knee breeches, lovat stockings, brogues, and a flat cap. She carried a shepherd's crook. The hair under the cap was grey, although he judged her to be in her forties. She had a face like a demented sheep.

She eyed Hamish up and down and then said, "Who's dead?"

"No one," said Hamish.

"Pity. My aunt Agnes is due to push up the daisies any day now and I am in her will. So what is it?"

"The fox."

She gave a bleating laugh. She is so like a sheep, thought Hamish.

"My dear Foxy," she said.

"You've been seen feeding the beast."

"So what?"

"So this, madam," said Hamish sternly. "Forget about your children's stories and Aesop's Fables.

Foxes are simply vermin like rats, but with one difference. It's the only animal I know that kills for pleasure. There are plenty of crofters in the Highlands who have found their newborn lambs with their throats ripped out and left to die. I am sure you want to settle in here and live peacefully with your neighbours. But if you continue to feed that wretched beast, God knows what will happen to you. One thing I am sure of, there will be a campaign to drive you out."

"I have a bond with Foxy," she said. "I am close to nature."

Was she mad? Hamish looked at her curiously. "You did know, when you bought this cottage, that there had been a murder here?"

"Of course. I got it for a very low price. Useful thing, murders." She laughed again, this time revealing large white teeth.

"I am warning you for the last time," said Hamish. "*Stop feeding that fox!*"

She slammed the door in his face.

As he drove back to Lochdubh, Hamish wondered whether to visit the Wright brothers to judge for himself whether they were afraid of anything. He decided to call on them. The funeral parlour was in Strathbane itself, the crematorium being situated outside the town.

A secretary ushered him into Mr. Kenneth Wright's office.

"What brings you here, Mr. Macbeth?" asked Kenneth.

He was wearing funereal black which accentuated the whiteness of his old face.

"Just this and that," said Hamish. "Mind if I sit down?"

Without waiting for a reply, he pulled forward a chair opposite Kenneth's desk. The walls of the little office were covered in photographs of funerals dating back to Edwardian times. The large mahogany desk boasted an antique silver-and-crystal inkwell. Sunlight shone through the dusty window above Kenneth's head onto the inkwell and sent harlequin sparkles of light across the desk.

"Would you care for some tea?" asked Kenneth as he raised a fine bone china cup to his purplish lips.

"I just wondered if anyone was frightening you," said Hamish bluntly.

Kenneth dropped the cup. It shattered and a pool of tea spread across the desk. He called, "Etty!" and the secretary came rushing in.

"Please clear this mess up, Etty," said Kenneth. "I am afraid I am very clumsy."

Hamish and Kenneth waited in silence while Etty mopped up the spilled tea with paper towels and then carefully gathered up the pieces of broken china.

"Will youse both be wanting tea?" asked Etty. She turned to Hamish. "Mr. Kenneth aye likes his lappysiching but I've got Tetley's."

"Mr. Macbeth is just leaving," said Kenneth.

"You haven't answered my question," said Hamish.

"Because it was a ridiculous question," said Kenneth. His shoulders were hunched and his head seemed to have shrunk down into his shirt.

"If it was a ridiculous question," said Hamish, "why are you afraid to answer it?"

"Show him out!" shouted Kenneth.

Etty was a small, plump girl with a round face. In the front of the funeral parlour, she threw the trash from the broken cup and spilled tea into a wastebasket and looked anxiously up at Hamish.

"Don't pay any heed to the auld man. He's aye flying aff the handle these days."

"Have you been working here long?"

"No, just the past few months," said Etty. "Afore me, it was some fellow, but he left to get a job in Glasgow. Cannae bring his name tae mind."

"Etty!" came Kenneth's voice.

"Gotta go," said Etty. "See ya."

Hamish drove slowly back to Lochdubh. He knew a retired locksmith who had previously skirted around the edges of the law. Perhaps he would visit him the next day and see if he could get a copy of Scully's keys. There might be something in the crematorium which might give him a clue.

At the police station, Hamish was preparing his

evening meal and tried not to miss Dick, who would have had dinner ready for him, the fire would have been lit in the living room, and they could have watched television together.

He fried two venison burgers and ate them with boiled potatoes washed down with a glass of water.

He had just finished when the phone rang. It was Dick.

"Are you getting on all right?" asked Dick. "No breakthrough?"

"Nothing. Although the funeral directors, the Wright brothers, seem scared about something. Gaunt used their crematorium for funerals."

"Well, if you need a break, come up here and we'll cook you a grand dinner."

Hamish had just rung off when someone knocked at the kitchen door. For a brief moment he forgot his pets were with Dick and looked to see if there was any warning reaction from them.

He opened the door to find Jimmy there.

"Man, you are in deep doo," said Jimmy, striding into the kitchen. "Got any whisky?"

Hamish immediately thought his idea of acting as bait had reached Strathbane. He put a bottle of whisky on the table and a glass. "What's up?" he asked.

"A mass demonstration in Strathbane the morrow by the Highlands and Islands Furry Friends Society."

"What's that got to do wi' me?"

"There's some mad biddy up at Cromish claiming you were howling about death to all foxes."

"Oh, for heffen's sakes," said Hamish exasperated. "There's this woman, Sam Trent, who's been feeding a fox and making a pet of it. So all the crofters round about are furious. A number of them probably lost lambs to this beast."

"Blair is making the most of it, oiling around Daviot and saying if you had shown a bit o' tact this wouldnae have happened."

"It'll all blow over," said Hamish. "I've never heard of this society."

"Well, you'll get to see them. You're to talk to the demonstration and say how sorry you are."

"This is madness, Jimmy! I cannae do that."

"Och, I'm sure that lot know bugger-all about foxes. Gie them a lecture."

In Cromish, Sam sat drinking at her kitchen table. She had left the door to the garden open in the hope of seeing the fox. She looked at the vodka bottle in front of her. She could not believe she had drunk so much. Maybe just a glass more. Then she would have a bath because she had spilled some stew over herself while staggering around the stove.

Samantha reflected drunkenly that she should really get to bed early to prepare for the long drive to Strathbane, where she would lead the demonstration. She had found the Highlands and Islands Furry Friends Society on the Internet and had told them about the horrible fox-hating policeman. To her delight, she was informed of the demonstration. She was just planning what to wear when she suddenly fell asleep, lolling back in her chair, her mouth open.

The large dog fox she had been feeding slunk silently into the kitchen, drawn by the smell of stew. Some of the stew had spilled onto Samantha's arm, and that arm was dangling near the floor, looking like a joint of meat.

It sank its teeth into that arm. The pain jerked Samantha awake. Terrified, she tried to beat the fox off. It wrenched a piece out of her arm and fled out the door.

Jimmy was just prepared to leave when the phone in the police station rang. Hamish went to answer it, saying over his shoulder, "You'd better wait in case it's for you."

He went into the office and closed the door.

When he came out, his face was grim.

"What's up?" asked Jimmy.

"That fox has just bitten a chunk out of that silly woman. Tell Strathbane. Dr. Williams has just called. She's been taken off to hospital in Strathbane. I'd better get down there and then do a report."

"If I were you, Hamish, I'd get onto the website of those Furry Friends and tell them. That'll kill that demo stone dead."

"I hope so," said Hamish. "But I call to mind a woman down in London who got bitten by an urban fox. The newspapers published her story. She got death threats from the animal libbers who seemed to think she had been cruel to the fox. Do you remember a few years ago when twin baby girls were left with arm and leg injuries after being attacked in their cots in their Hackney home? Then there was that poor wee baby boy, only four months, pulled from the sofa in his home by a fox and dragged out into the garden. He suffered injuries to his hand and face and a finger was almost severed. Mind you, that was London again where the townies will feed foxes."

"And here endeth the first lesson," said Jimmy. "Let's get going."

Chapter Eleven

Look here. Upon my soul you mustn't come into the place saying you want to know, you know.

—*Charles Dickens*

"I hope she gets rabies shots, the silly cow," said Jimmy as he and Hamish sat outside the hospital room where Samantha Trent lay, waiting for permission to speak to her.

"Shouldn't think so," said Hamish. "Foxes aren't known to be rabid. The trouble wi' foxes is they look right handsome and folk think of fairy stories and all that. If they looked like cockroaches, nobody would think twice of killing them. It's survival of the cutest. I doubt if she'll stay on in Cromish after all this."

A doctor approached them. "Miss Trent is sedated but you can have a few words with her."

"How is her arm?" asked Hamish.

"Badly damaged but the surgeons managed to save it."

"You go in," said Jimmy. "What are we wasting time on this silly woman for?"

Hamish entered the room where Samantha lay with her eyes closed, her arm thick with bandages.

She stared miserably at Hamish. "I'm going back to Edinburgh. This would never have happened in Edinburgh."

"It might," said Hamish. "There are urban foxes."

A tear rolled down her cheek. Hamish dabbed it with a tissue. He felt a great wave of pity for her.

"Try to get some sleep," he said. "Can I get you anything? Magazines or books?"

"A magazine, maybe."

"A wildlife one?"

"No. Get me *People's Friend*. I want to read silly romantic stories and forget about every damn animal on the planet."

Hamish went out to join Jimmy. "Talk some sense into her?" asked Jimmy.

"I'm right sorry for her. Okay, she's a daft romantic. But what would the world be without romantics? Where would some of the rarer species be today if folk didn't care about them? I'm off to get her a magazine."

"And I'm off to my bed," grumbled Jimmy. "What a waste of time!"

When Hamish returned to Samantha's room, she had fallen asleep. He left the magazine beside the bed.

The following day was fine with a frisky wind. Hamish felt restless. Never before had he been left with so many unsolved murders. The Wright brothers were afraid. Their funeral parlour was in a busy street, but the crematorium was more isolated.

He drove over to Bonar Bridge where he knew former burglar Alex Cromarty lived. Alex was old now and bent over with gnarled arthritic hands, but he said if Hamish gave him an hour, he could make keys from the impressions.

His thoughts turned to Samantha. The far north of Scotland could come as a shock to incomers. A lot of people could not grasp the idea that the people in the Highlands were a different race from the lowlanders.

Certainly most were rightly famous for courtesy and hospitality. But there were the other types: malicious, petty, and vengeful.

The sky above was turning light grey and the wind was freshening. A storm was forecast.

He returned and collected the set of keys and paid for them.

As he approached the police station, he saw Christine Dalray standing outside. He mostly had seen her wearing her forensic whites, apart from that one date. But she was wearing high heels and a short skirt showing excellent legs.

"Can I help?" asked Hamish when he got down from the Land Rover.

"If it's not too late, I thought I'd take you for lunch," said Christine.

"That would be grand. Do you want to wait until I change?"

"No, you're fine as you are."

Hamish heard the phone in the police station ringing. "I'd better get that, Christine," he said. "Won't be long."

It was Priscilla. "Where are you?" asked Hamish.

"London. How is everything?"

"Not very good." Hamish suddenly wondered whether the police station phone was bugged. He said, "I've just found out where the loot the murderer has hidden is stashed."

"Where?"

"I cannae tell ye over the phone," said Hamish. "I'm keeping the news to myself for the moment. I want to score one over Blair."

"I'll be coming up next week," said Priscilla. "Maybe we'll have dinner together."

"Let me know when you arrive."

Hamish rang off and went out to join Christine. "Where are your pets?" she asked as they walked along the waterfront.

"Having a holiday wi' Dick."

"Do you miss Dick?"

"I've got used to my own company again," said Hamish.

In the restaurant, Willie Lamont fussed about them, finding a table at the window.

"So is there any news at all?" asked Christine.

"Not a thing," said Hamish gloomily.

Priscilla, too, was having lunch. Paul Dubois, the attractive Frenchman who had stayed at the Tommel Castle Hotel, had phoned up to invite her.

When they were seated in Rules restaurant in Covent Garden, he talked about his wine business. Then he said, "There was news of awful murders when I was up north. Anyone found anything?"

"I just spoke to my friend, Hamish Macbeth, the local police sergeant. He's playing at being the Lone Ranger again."

"In what way?"

"Evidently the murderer or murderers had hidden something valuable. He's found out where it is, but he's not telling his bosses. He wants to produce it himself and get all the kudos."

"Excuse me," said Paul.

Priscilla waited for his return—and waited. But the handsome Frenchman never came back.

She returned to the office but could not settle down to her work. What did she know of Dubois? And why had he rushed off after she had told him about Hamish?

At last, she phoned Elspeth Grant and told her about her broken lunch date and about Hamish saying that he knew where the loot was stashed.

"He'll get himself killed," said Elspeth. "Strathbane will need to be told."

"If I do that, he'll never speak to me again," said Priscilla. "Dubois was in London. What can he do?"

"He can get a plane to Inverness and drive like the clappers to Lochdubh," said Elspeth. "I know. I'll phone Dick."

Hamish meanwhile was wondering what was up with him. Christine was attractive and intelligent, and yet he did not fancy her. He suddenly wanted the meal to be over and when Christine said it was her day off and they could spend the afternoon together, he said, "There's a big storm coming up. You'd better leave for Strathbane or you might not get back."

She looked disappointed, but when they left the restaurant and walked back to where she had parked her car, the wind was shrieking along the waterfront and choppy waves on the loch were crashing down on the shingle beach.

Hamish rather sadly watched her go. He decided that her lack of attraction for him was caused by the buildup of nerves he was feeling at the thought of breaking into the crematorium.

At one in the morning, he almost decided to call the whole thing off. The storm was raging in its fury. Thunder crashed overhead. But he realised that the storm was good cover. No one would be out on a night like this.

There are few trees in Sutherland, but two of them had managed to become uprooted and block the road to Strathbane and he had to bump the Land Rover round over the moor to get past them. Great buffets of wind tore at his vehicle, and lightning lit up the sky. It was as if the whole countryside was involved in a hellish dance.

Hamish parked at the back of the crematorium. Bending before the wind, he made it to the side door that Scully had used.

He opened the door and let himself in. He silently made his way to Kenneth Wright's office. He searched through all the papers on and in the desk without finding anything incriminating.

He made his way to the coffin store. He searched coffin after coffin, his pencil torch flickering from one to the other. He stopped abruptly at one point. He sensed something. But he could not hear anything sinister because of the noise of the storm.

Scully was awakened from a peaceful sleep. The call was from a girl he had met in the rehab. "I was coming back frae a club in Inverness," she said. "I saw a wee light in the crematorium. Maybe you've got burglars."

"I'll go and hae a look," said Scully.

"Aren't you going to call the police?"

"Aye. O' course."

But Scully had no intention of calling the police. That awful man Blair might turn up. Scully had met him before on one of the times he had been caught with drugs. Blair had punched him in the face.

He dressed hurriedly, got onto his scooter, and set off for the crematorium.

"He must be somewhere," Dick was saying to Anka. "He's not at the police station and the Land Rover's gone." Anka sat beside him, cradling a deer rifle. "Do you know how to use that?" asked Dick.

"Yes," said Anka. "Listen, Dick. Let's try Strathbane. Don't you remember Hamish said something once about the funeral people being frightened?"

"Right," said Dick. "Let's try there."

Hamish sat down on a coffin to think. There was an idea at the back of his mind. He had seen something. What was it?

A dark shape materialised from the shadows of the room and a voice said, "Get your hands up!"

Hamish rose slowly to his feet. A flash of lightning lit up the coffin store and he recognised Paul Dubois holding a gun, and beside him a small tattooed man.

"Where's the stuff?" demanded Dubois.

"I haven't the faintest idea," said Hamish.

"Laurent! Put a coffin on that gurney over there," ordered Dubois.

He waited until the coffin was loaded onto the gurney. Then he said, "Get into the coffin. I am going to help you remember."

"It won't do you any good," said Hamish.

"We'll see. Get in."

Anything to play for time, thought Hamish.

He lowered himself into the coffin. Dubois stood over him.

"Now, *mon ami*, this is what is going to happen. We will take you to the cliffs. I will ask you again. If you persist in lying, you and this coffin will be thrown over the cliffs and into the sea. Where is my stuff?"

"I don't know. I tell you I really don't know," shouted Hamish.

"Screw the coffin down, Laurent," said Dubois. "Search him first. Take his belt. Xavier has the hearse outside. Load this bastard in."

Hamish made a sudden upwards lunge but Laurent brought a heavy pistol crashing down on the side of his head and Hamish slumped back into the coffin.

Scully parked his scooter some way away from the crematorium. He planned to creep up on the place; if there was a burglar, he would put an anonymous call to the police. He had tried to call Hamish but had not received any reply.

He assumed someone was maybe trying to thieve the computers or looking for cash. Maybe a drug addict.

That would be odd, he thought: an ex-druggie catching a functioning one.

The storm had raced away to the east. There was a final distant rumble of thunder. A small moon appeared to race high above through the ragged clouds.

Scully heard a noise and crouched down behind a laurel bush and peered through its branches. Two men were sliding a coffin off a gurney into a hearse while a tall man stood watching.

"I hope you haven't killed Macbeth," he heard the tall man say. "I need him to talk."

Scully shivered with fear. If he phoned the police from his mobile, they would trace the call to him.

Then he heard the tall man say, "We'll take him to the cliffs outside Lochdubh."

"He may not know anything," said one of the men.

"Then just throw him into the sea," said the tall man.

Scully crept away. He decided to get to the cliffs by a circuitous route and, on the way, he would call the police from a phone box.

Hamish's head ached. He could feel the hearse moving at a slow pace. He wondered how soon the air in the coffin would run out. Hadn't they thought he might die of lack of oxygen? They had taken his duty belt with his stun gun, phone, flashlight, baton, and handcuffs. But he had a Swiss army knife in his pocket. He slowly eased it out and felt desperately for the small saw contained amongst the various knives.

Hoping the noise of the engine would cover the sound of sawing, he attacked the side of the coffin. He could not turn on his side, but fear and desperation seemed to be lending almost robotic strength to his hand. He finally achieved a small hole. He then selected the strongest knife. He would try his best to kill Dubois.

Dick was driving the bakery van. He pulled to a stop in front of one of the fallen trees on the Strathbane road. He groaned. "I'd better get out and try to move it. I'll break this van's chassis if I try to go off-road."

He and Anka were struggling with the tree when they heard a vehicle approaching from the Strathbane side. Anka shielded her eyes against the approaching vehicle's headlights.

"It's a hearse, Dick. I don't like this."

The hearse stopped on the other side of the tree and two men got out. They joined Dick and Anka and together they hauled the tree to the side of the road.

Dick recognised the tattooed man from identikit pictures that had been posted in all the papers.

"What's a hearse doing out this time of night?" he asked.

A tall man loomed up in the headlights. "It is an order from relatives of the deceased at the Tommel Castle Hotel."

Hamish heard the voices. If he cried out, then whoever it was would probably be shot.

Dick and Anka got into the bakery van. "I'll let them get ahead," he said. "This road only leads to Lochdubh. I recognised one of them. He's wanted for murder. I'll switch off the lights. Don't worry, I know this road well. Here's Jimmy Anderson's home number. Tell him we think the murderers have got Hamish."

Scully had already made his phone call. He called Strathbane headquarters instead of dialling 999. The policeman who received it thought it important enough to phone Blair at home. Blair listened. He thought that if it were true, then he would be rid of Macbeth for once and for all. "Forget it, laddie," he said. "Who called?"

"Anonymous caller."

"There you are. Load of rubbish."

"Who was that?" asked Blair's wife, Mary, when he had rung off.

"Just some nutcase," said Blair, and with a happy smile on his face he went back to sleep.

In the streetlights of Lochdubh, from his vantage point on the bridge leading into the village, Dick could make out the hearse going through the village and out the other side.

"They're going to the cliffs," said Dick. "Phone Jimmy again. I'll park at the end and we'll go up on foot."

Hamish heard the lid of the coffin being unscrewed. When the lid was lifted, he sat up groggily. His head hurt from where he had been struck. The noise of the great Atlantic waves pounding the cliffs was loud in his ears. The coffin was loaded out onto the gurney.

"For the last time," said Dubois, "where is my stuff?"

"I don't know," said Hamish. "I really don't know. If I knew where your stuff was I'd shove it up your arse."

Laurent said something in thickly accented French.

Dubois replied in English, "No, I don't think torture would do us any good. I am convinced he really doesn't know. Xavier, screw the lid down again and throw the coffin over."

Scully, lying hidden in the heather, suddenly decided he couldn't bear it. He owed his life to Hamish Macbeth.

He stood up and shouted "Stop! I am making a citizen's arrest."

A torch was shone in his face.

"Get him," said Dubois. "Throw him over."

"Run, Scully!" shouted Hamish.

But Scully was seized. "Hold him there," said Dubois. "He can follow Macbeth." He strolled to the edge of the cliff and looked down into the heaving water.

Now, even in the rehab where they talked about a Higher Power, Scully was an unbeliever. But there are no agnostics on the battlefield and Scully shouted, "Damn your black soul to hell! God will punish you!"

And then everything seemed to happen at once.

A giant wave rose above the cliff. Scully was to say later that it was as if great watery fingers had seized Dubois and dragged him screaming over the edge. Laurent fled across the moors. Xavier was howling because Hamish had stabbed him in the neck. A police helicopter sailed overhead, lighting up the scene.

Clutching his neck, Xavier started to run down the brae, but Anka and Dick saw him. Dick brought him down with a rugby tackle and Anka sat on him.

Hamish tried to struggle out of the coffin. Laurent was fleeing away from the direction of the village over the moors. But Hamish's struggles set the gurney in motion. As it hurtled down the hill, he clutched desperately at the sides as a pale dawn broke over the scene.

Jimmy, driving into Lochdubh at the head of a line of police cars, braked hard as Hamish Macbeth, sitting up in a coffin, sped past him, right over the harbour wall and into the loch.

Archie Maclean, the fisherman, who had been unable to go out because of the gale, was sitting on a bollard as Hamish shot past into the loch. He detached a life belt from the side of the harbour wall and sent it sailing in the direction where Hamish had gone under.

Police got out of their cars. Jimmy shouted to them to get up to the cliff. He waited anxiously. He had almost given up hope when Hamish's head rose above the choppy waters of the loch.

Hamish clutched the life belt and slowly made his way to the harbour steps, where he was helped up by Jimmy and Archie.

"Get him into the station," ordered Jimmy, "and get Dr. Brodie to have a look at him. Can you speak, Hamish? What's happened?"

Hamish summoned up strength to lie. He could not say he had broken into the crematorium, so he said he had received an anonymous call that there were lights in the crematorium and had gone to investigate.

"The head man, Paul Dubois, is dead," he said. "A wave washed him out to sea. The tattooed man has fled. Dick and Anka have got one of the gang, but the other one has escaped."

"I'll get the rest from you later," said Jimmy.

Judging that the police car would not get up to the top of the cliffs, Jimmy set off on foot.

Hamish was surrounded by villagers who had been roused from their beds by the commotion. Mr. Patel wrapped Hamish in a fleecy blanket, and he was led to the police station.

Dr. Brodie appeared and examined Hamish's head and then phoned for an ambulance. "It's off to hospital with you to get that head scanned."

Hamish protested weakly that he was fine but Brodie said it was a hard blow and he might have bleeding from the brain.

Up on the cliffs, Xavier was being taken away to hospital. The cut on his neck had missed the main artery, but Jimmy wanted him fit and well for the interrogation to come.

Dick told Jimmy how Scully had tried to save Hamish's life. "It was right weird," said Dick. "One moment Scully was calling down the wrath of God on that Frenchman, and the next this enormous wave just rose up and snatched him off into the sea."

Jimmy turned to Scully. "Did you phone the police?"

"I phoned the station in Strathbane and spoke to some policeman," said Scully.

"I didn't hear anything about it until I heard that Anka here had phoned."

"Well, I did," said Scully.

"I want you to come back to headquarters and make your statement," said Jimmy.

In hospital later that day, Hamish was relieved to find he would not need an operation. He was suffering from concussion. He had been miserably sick and then he fell into a nightmare-ridden sleep where he was back in the crematorium, his pencil torch flickering around Kenneth Wright's office. When he woke, he felt better and found Dick by his bedside.

Dick told him about remembering that Hamish had said the Wright brothers were afraid of something, and about how Elspeth had phoned with news from Priscilla that a man called Dubois had left her alone in a restaurant after she had said that Hamish knew where the goods were stashed.

"And do you know?" came Jimmy's voice from behind Dick.

"I don't know. I don't know why I said that," said Hamish.

"Right, I am here to take your statement. Wait outside, Dick."

Jimmy switched on a tape recorder and said, "Begin at the beginning."

As Hamish talked, he began to worry about Kenneth and Robert Wright. If they had been involved in any way, then someone had threatened them. Why?

He stopped talking and gazed vacantly at Jimmy. He was back in his dream, back in Kenneth's office.

He sat up suddenly. "Switch that off, Jimmy, and get me out o' here. I think I do know where the stuff is."

"Tell me!"

"No, I want to see for myself."

*   *   *

Blair woke late that morning. It was his day off. He was turning over to go back to sleep when his wife, Mary, came into the room.

"It's all over the telly," she said. "You should see it. Film o' Hamish Macbeth in a coffin landing in the loch."

That enterprising shopkeeper, Mr. Patel, had filmed the whole thing on his mobile phone and sold the film to the networks.

Blair shot out of bed and padded through to the living room in time to see Scully on the television. "It was the hand of God," Scully was saying as he stood on the steps of police headquarters. Blair listened appalled as Scully went on to tell how he had been told there were lights at the crematorium where he worked and how he had heard they planned to throw Hamish Macbeth off the cliffs. This was followed by grainy footage of Hamish in his coffin, hurtling down the hill and into the loch.

Blair began to sweat. Who was that policeman who had called him? He remembered it was that new recruit, Todd Judson. He'd better try to find him and promise him promotion, anything, to keep his mouth shut. If he was on the night shift, he'd be at home now. He phoned the duty officer and got Todd's home address.

*   *   *

But Todd had seen the television report while he was having his breakfast, and, determined to be part of it all, even in a small way, he made his way to police headquarters. Also, Blair had told him to forget it and he didn't want to find himself accused of not passing on vital information.

But most of the force were out in the search for Laurent. Todd wanted to share a little bit of the excitement, so when he saw Daviot striding in, he waylaid him and said, "Should I put in a report about my call to Mr. Blair?"

"What call?"

"I got an anonymous call last night that some villains at the crematorium had loaded Hamish Macbeth into a coffin and were going to throw him into the sea."

"Good lad. But I am surprised Mr. Blair did not go to the cliffs himself."

"He told me to forget it," said Todd. "He said it was probably some nutter. Should I put in a report, sir?"

At that moment Blair came rushing in. He saw Todd with the superintendent and turned to flee. But Daviot shouted, "Blair! My office. Now!"

At the crematorium, Kenneth and Robert Wright were standing outside, complaining that a forensic team had refused them admittance.

"Are you sure about this?" Jimmy asked Hamish.

"I'd better be," said Hamish.

Jimmy went in, followed by Hamish. As he made his way to Kenneth's office, Christine appeared and said, "You can't go in there. We haven't processed it yet."

Hamish brushed past her. "This is important."

He stood with his hands on his hips and surveyed the line of urns on the shelf behind Kenneth's desk.

He walked forward and took one down. The top of the urn had a waxed seal. Hamish took out a penknife and sliced the seal.

"I hope to God you're right!" said Jimmy.

Hamish carried the urn forward. "Look at this!"

"White powder. I'll be damned." Jimmy stuck a finger in the powder and tasted it. "If I'm not mistaken, this is pure cocaine. I'll get the brothers in here."

He returned with Kenneth and Robert. They looked at the opened urn.

"He made us do it," cried Kenneth. "He said he'd kill us if we said anything. He said he'd kill my granddaughter as well."

"Who?" demanded Hamish. "Was it Gaunt?"

Kenneth and Robert nodded their old heads in unison.

"But when you learned of his murder," said Jimmy, "why didn't you come forward?"

"He said he was the head of an international gang,"

said Robert. Tears began to run down the wrinkles on his face. "I thought the others would come for us. Is it all over now?"

"Are all these urns full of the drugs?" asked Hamish.

"Yes," said Kenneth. "Will we go to jail?"

"No," said Hamish. "It's all over now."

Jimmy phoned Daviot with the news. "Brilliant work," said Daviot. "I will inform the press."

He turned to the cringing figure of Blair. "I will decide what to do with you later. Anderson and Macbeth have just found an enormous haul of cocaine."

He swept from the room. Blair hurried after him.

Daviot knew the press were massed outside headquarters. He smoothed back his hair and went outside to make an announcement, unaware that Blair had followed him.

Flashes went off and cameras rolled as he told the media about the find of the cocaine.

"I am very proud of our officers," said Daviot at the end of his speech. "But one of the men is still at large. We only know him by the name of Laurent. You have the identikit picture and I would be grateful if you could feature it again."

A reporter called out, "Have you anything to add, Chief Inspector Blair?"

Daviot swung round. Blair gave him an oily smile.

"It was all down to the organising genius of Superintendent Daviot," he said. "He is the hero of the day."

And that was how Blair kept his job. Daviot had been about to give Hamish Macbeth the credit. But, he thought quickly, Macbeth was a maverick. It was in the interests of the police force that he should take all the credit.

Chapter Twelve

☠

The bright face of danger.

—*Robert Louis Stevenson*

If I were starring in a television detective drama, thought Hamish Macbeth sourly, the credits would be rolling and that would be that. But here I am, writing out reams and reams of reports. Begin at the beginning, Macbeth. What happened when you went to the crematorium? How did you guess where the cocaine was hidden? Please submit all reports in triplicate. And while he typed and typed at the police station computer, he felt sourly that he was being kept out of the loop. There was bad news. Xavier had got ahold of drugs in hospital and had committed suicide, so Hamish had to send report after report as to why he had stabbed the man.

There was a countrywide search for the tattooed man called Laurent. Hamish tried several times to phone Jimmy but was always told the detective was too busy to answer his calls. The sad fact was that

Jimmy felt Hamish had received enough glory; he wanted to be the one who caught Laurent.

The press had given up trying to contact Hamish because Hamish had been ordered by Daviot to let headquarters handle all the media reports. Hamish was surprised that Superintendent Douglas had not phoned or called, not knowing that Douglas had been told that the police sergeant was recovering from the attack on him and was not to be disturbed. He was just sending off his final report when Priscilla walked into the police station.

"I am so sorry, Hamish," she said. "You would never have been attacked if I hadn't told Dubois you knew where the drugs were."

"You're forgiven," said Hamish. "I was setting myself up as bait anyway. But the mad greed o' the man! All he had to do was wait until the end of the meal."

"I don't think he was French at all," said Priscilla.

"Why?"

"When he was staying at the hotel, we were talking to some of the guests and they asked him if he was from Quebec. He was usually polite but he snapped at them that he had never, ever been there."

"We should ha' guessed that," said Hamish ruefully. "Gaunt came from Canada, as did the Leighs. I think Dubois, if that's his real name, used small-time villains like the Leighs, or Southerns as their real name was, to get the drugs out with the help of Gaunt."

"Never mind. I'm sure Interpol or the Canadian police are on to that. I'll take you for a soothing lunch. Does your head hurt?"

A patch of Hamish's red hair had been shaved and a plaster put on the wound.

"Not now. Let's go. I'm sick o' this computer."

"Where are Sonsie and Lugs?"

"Still with Dick. I'm going to Braikie tomorrow to pick them up."

They walked together along the waterfront. From the security of a rented car, Blair watched them go.

Earlier that morning, Daviot had been landed with a suggestion from Police Scotland to close down the station in Lochdubh. He knew he would have to refuse, for Hamish held that incriminating photo of his wife. During a previous case, his wife had been drugged and photographed in a very compromising situation. Hamish had recovered the photograph and negatives for Daviot but had kept one back. He had told his boss that if his police station was closed down, then he would send copies of that dreadful photograph to all the newspapers.

Actually, Hamish knew that when it came to the crunch, he would do no such thing.

But with that photograph in Hamish's possession, Daviot felt vulnerable. He sent for Blair.

Blair came in, looking like a whipped dog.

"I want you to do me a favour," said Daviot. "You owe me. Remember, I still have the power to fire you."

"Anything I can do, I will do," said Blair. "Anything for you, sir."

"Macbeth has an incriminating photo of my wife." He quickly told Blair how Hamish had come by it and how he could not close down the police station until he got that photo back.

"Leave it wi' me, sir," said Blair. "I know where he keeps the key to the station. I'll watch when he goes out and I'll get it for ye."

So Blair waited until he saw Priscilla and Hamish going into the restaurant and drove to the police station. As he was well known in Lochdubh, he knew none of the villagers would think his visit odd.

He searched in the gutter above the kitchen door and grunted with satisfaction when his fingers found the key. Before opening the door, Blair listened hard. By asking around, he had found out that Hamish's pets were still with Dick.

He let himself in and got to work in the office, jerking open drawers in Hamish's desk and spilling the contents onto the floor. A bottom drawer was locked.

He went out to a shed where he knew Hamish kept his tools and returned with a chisel. He broke the lock, upended the drawer, and began to rifle through the contents of bankbooks, birth certificate, family photographs, and a small box containing an engagement ring. Then he saw that a manila envelope was pasted onto the bottom of the drawer. He ripped it open and let out a low whistle. The photograph of Mrs. Daviot at last.

He seized it and fled the police station.

Archie Maclean, the fisherman, had been on his road to the station with two fish for Hamish when he saw Blair's flight. Alarmed, he hurried to the station and found the door open. He went in, calling, "Hamish!"

Then he saw the office door was open and the mess of papers on the floor. He hurried out and went into Patel's shop. "Anyone seen Hamish?" he shouted.

"I saw him go past with Miss Priscilla," said Patel.

The restaurant, thought Archie.

He ran along the waterfront and erupted into the restaurant.

"Blair's broken into your station and there are papers all over the floor."

"Wait here," said Hamish to Priscilla.

"No, I'm coming with you." The three of them ran along the waterfront to the station.

The first thing Hamish saw in his office was that upturned drawer with an empty manila envelope stuck to the bottom.

"He's got the photo," said Hamish.

*   *   *

Later that afternoon, Daviot looked uneasily at Blair. "You are sure you've got it?"

"Yes, it's safe and sound wi' me. I could be doing wi' a wee dram."

Daviot gave him an outraged look which Blair returned with a fat smile. He's going to blackmail me until the ends of time, thought Daviot, and there's nothing I can do about it.

At the same time, Mary, Blair's wife, was lifting up the mattress on their bed. She had crept to the door of the bedroom earlier on when her husband had returned and had wondered why he was being so furtive.

She picked up the photograph and scowled at it. Mary did not have very good eyesight, but she did not even bother to put on her glasses. All she knew was that it was a pornographic photograph. Her husband's drunkenness was enough but she wasn't going to have him leering over porn.

Mary took the photograph through to the fireplace, threw it in, struck a match, and watched it burn.

The phone rang. "Hullo, Hamish," said Mary, who felt she owed the police sergeant a lot. For hadn't Hamish cleverly got her off the streets and into marriage with Blair? Other women might find Blair a horrible man, but Mary loved her home and respectable position and knew how to handle her husband.

"Your husband stole an important piece of evidence, a photo, from my station," said Hamish.

"You mean thon dirty photo? I didn't know it was evidence," said Mary. "I burnt the thing."

Hamish began to laugh. "You're a grand girl, Mary. Did you know who was in the photo?"

"No, some tart getting shagged."

"Forget about it," said Hamish.

Archie had gone. But Priscilla had heard the story. "Why didn't he send it straight to Daviot?" she asked. "Why did you think to phone his wife?"

"Because," said Hamish, "a man like Blair would immediately think of the power that photo gave him over the boss. Poor Mr. Daviot. I'll ring up and put him out of his misery."

"You and I are like brithers," Blair was saying expansively when the phone rang. Daviot's secretary, Helen, said, "It's that man Macbeth on the phone. I told him you weren't available but he said it was urgent."

"Put him on," ordered Daviot.

"I will be as brief as possible, sir," said Hamish. "You sent Blair to break into my police station and steal that photograph. He hid it under the mattress at his home, where his wife found it. She did not recognise the subject. She thought it was porn and so she burnt it. You sent Blair. He did not wear gloves. I can charge him. Knowing that scunner, he will immediately start blabbing that he did it on your orders. You should recognise real loyalty and stop trying to close my station down."

"Thank you, Hamish," said Daviot meekly. Blair slowly put down his glass. When Daviot said Hamish instead of Macbeth, it meant he was pleased with him.

"You silly drunken fool," said Daviot evenly. "You didn't wear gloves and now Macbeth has your fingerprints and evidence from the locals that you are guilty of burglary."

Blair grinned. "You'd better get him to hush it up. It isnae my arse that's on the line."

"Stand up when you are addressing me!" roared Daviot. "Your wife found where you had hidden it, and thinking it was porn she burnt it."

Blair turned a muddy colour.

"So get out of here and never, ever try to blackmail me again."

"I wasnae…"

"Get out!"

When Blair had gone, Daviot phoned Hamish. "Send me a bill for any damage," he said. "Is there anything else I can do?"

"Just be extra nice to Mary Blair. She puts up with a lot. Did Mr. Blair try to blackmail you, sir?"

"Not in so many words, but the implication was there."

"Don't worry, sir," said Hamish. "I should ha' never kept thon photo."

"As I live and breathe," said Daviot, "you will keep your station."

After he had run off, Daviot called Helen in and, to her dismay, began to dictate a long letter explaining why the Lochdubh station must be kept open.

When Hamish had finished the call, Priscilla looked at him doubtfully. "I've got a nasty feeling that you're as bad as Blair, hanging on to that photograph."

"Sutherland needs a man like me on the beat," said Hamish stubbornly. He was suddenly weary of the oh-so-beautiful, oh-so-untouchable Priscilla. "Come here and give me a kiss," he said.

"Don't be silly," said Priscilla. "I have got to go."

Blair erupted into his home and began yelling and shouting at his wife. Mary stared at him when she heard the photo had been that of Mrs. Daviot, "Okay, she was drugged and framed," shouted Blair, "but I could ha' got anything out o' Daviot I wanted. I'm going to gie you the thrashing you deserve." He raised his fists and advanced on her.

Mary kicked him in the balls. Blair fell to the floor, groaning and writhing. His wife put on her coat and went out to do some shopping. Sometimes, she thought ruefully, husbands like hers were really hard work.

*   *   *

The days slid past with no sighting of the elusive Laurent. Hamish began to think that he had maybe bribed someone up the coast to take him off in a boat.

He missed Elspeth. He wanted to discuss the case with her and see if that odd intuition of hers could come up with anything. He was just reaching for the phone to call her when he heard a familiar voice calling, "Hamish!"

He went through to the kitchen and there was Elspeth, smiling at him.

"I was chust about to phone you," said Hamish, the strengthening of his accent showing how excited he was at seeing her. "What brings you?"

"Another crime documentary," said Elspeth. "The last one sold well in America. I feel like a fraud. A team of researchers does most of the work and I just stand there in front of the camera with my arms folded, looking stern. I've been to Strathbane and done all the interviews. I'm afraid I haven't got permission to interview you."

"Doesn't matter," said Hamish. "Have you any free time? I'd like to pick your brains."

"Yes. What do you want to do?"

"It's a grand day. Let's go for a drive. I'll take Sonsie and Lugs. They need the exercise. I think Dick fed them too many cakes and buns."

Elspeth noticed how the animals had come to accept her. It's almost as if they realise I am no threat, she thought. They all climbed into the Land Rover.

"I thought you weren't supposed to take private passengers," said Elspeth.

"Nobody's bothering about me," said Hamish. "Where shall we go?"

"Anywhere," said Elspeth happily.

"I know," said Hamish. "We'll go up to Cromish." He told her about the fox-loving Samantha. "I just want to make sure she's all right. I feel sorry for her."

When they got to Cromish, Hamish thought that Samantha had perhaps left and was surprised to find her at home: not only at home, but changed in appearance for the better. She had put on weight and her cheeks were rosy.

And she was wearing a sparkling diamond ring on her engagement finger.

"Who's the lucky man?" asked Hamish.

"I'm going to be married to Dr. Williams," said Samantha.

"How did that happen?" asked Hamish when they were seated in Samantha's kitchen.

"When I got out of hospital," said Samantha, "I was a neurotic mess and went to him for anti-depressants. He said all I had to do was to accept country life, eat more, and get exercise. He sort of took me over." She laughed happily.

"And what about the fox?" asked Elspeth.

"I haven't seen him. Harold, that's Dr. Williams, took me all round the crofts and got the crofters to tell me horrible stories about foxes."

Hamish found it hard to believe the transformation. He would have expected such as Samantha to go back to Edinburgh and spend her time on the Internet connecting up with animal libbers.

When they left her, Hamish suggested they buy some stuff from the shop and have a picnic on the beach.

"Now *this*," said Elspeth, "is what I call the best bacon bap in Scotland."

"She's missing Anka. But Mrs. Mackay always had a grand hand wi' the baps."

Little waves hissed up on the hard white sand, and Sonsie and Lugs raced up and down chasing seagulls.

Hamish told Elspeth all about the case and then said, "What puzzles me is how this Laurent can escape detection when he's got a Quebec accent and a tattooed face. He can bleach his hair and do all sorts of things but he can't get rid o' thae tattoos. Any ideas?"

Elspeth frowned as she concentrated hard. Hamish watched her face affectionately. If only, if only, he thought.

"I know. He could black it up. He's probably got all sorts of forged identities. He could have moved to Glasgow or London where no one would notice another black face. But they're rare in the Highlands. We've got Indians and Pakistanis, but they're brown.

"If he's clever, he won't want to have moved much away from the Highlands. Police are thin on the ground in the north of Scotland. Did the police manage to get a photo of him from Canada?"

"Not that I've heard. Laurent is probably not his real name."

"What about fingerprints?"

"He wore gloves."

"Here's an idea," said Elspeth. "Have you one of the identikit pictures?"

"Aye, I've one at the station."

"They're running a trailer for this crime programme tonight. We could change his face to black, photograph it, and I could e-mail it in with instructions to show it on the trailer. You won't get into trouble. I'll say I thought of it myself."

"I'd like to catch the man myself," said Hamish. "But phone calls will go straight to the police."

"No they won't. I'll give instructions with a number that they are to call the television station and tell the station to call me at the Tommel Castle Hotel. I'll tell them that we might get an exclusive that way. I'll pass anything on to you."

"What time will it be broadcast?"

"Every hour on the hour this evening. Let's get back to the station and get started."

*   *   *

People might complain about immigrants to the British Isles, but Hamish thought that surely shopkeepers like Mr. Patel were God's gift. He seemed to stock everything and that included a bottle of india ink and brushes.

Back at the station, they turned Laurent's face black and waited for the ink to dry. Then, after a long consultation with her boss, Elspeth took several photographs and e-mailed them over.

"You'd better come up to the hotel with me," she said, "and be on hand if there is any news."

Elspeth was irritated to find that Hamish was taking Sonsie and Lugs with him. She often felt the man was married to his pets. But Hamish took the animals through to the hotel kitchen and left them with the chef before returning to join Elspeth in the bar.

They watched the television programme on Elspeth's computer. At six o'clock, the trailer came on and Laurent's blackened face appeared.

"Let's hope we get something soon," fretted Hamish. "Strathbane will be on to your station, demanding that any calls be routed to them."

"I thought of that," said Elspeth, "and told them to stall the police for as long as possible."

They waited until seven o'clock and watched the trailer again. The bar was filling up.

"Let's go up to my room," suggested Elspeth.

They sat moodily, staring at the screen, waiting and waiting, too nervous to speak.

Elspeth's phone suddenly rang, making both of them jump. "We've got some calls," came her boss, Barry's, voice. Elspeth pressed the loudspeaker button on her phone so that Hamish could hear the messages as well.

The first one claimed that Laurent was working as a dishwasher in a restaurant in Glasgow. Hamish shook his head. Laurent would not take any job where the black would run off his hands.

The second was from a hysterical woman, claiming that Laurent was the husband who had deserted her.

The third, a man claiming Laurent owed him money.

"That's all for now," said Barry. "We might get something later."

"I hope he hasn't just taken someone hostage in their house," said Hamish.

The phone rang half an hour later. They listened, but without much hope. Hamish suddenly stiffened. A restaurateur in Golspie, called Hugo Bryan, claimed that the identikit looked like his maître d', who was called Felix Dejeux. The restaurant was called The Fine Fish.

Elspeth took a note of the phone number, which she handed to Hamish.

Hamish called the restaurant owner and explained who he was. "When do you close?" he asked.

"Eleven thirty," said Bryan.

"I'll be right over," said Hamish. "Does he wear gloves?"

"No."

"Anyway, I'll be there and don't do anything to make him suspicious."

He turned to Elspeth. "He isn't wearing gloves."

"We forgot," said Elspeth. "There's such things as indelible dye. I'll get my camera crew and follow you over."

"Don't do that," said Hamish sharply. "It could be dangerous."

"If it weren't for me," shouted Elspeth, "you wouldn't have got this tip-off."

Hamish realised he was wasting time arguing. He left the hotel by way of the kitchen, shouting to Clarry, the chef, to look after his animals.

Golspie is a village in Sutherland, lying on the North Sea coast in the shadow of Ben Bhraggie. It has a population about fifteen hundred. Hamish remembered that The Fine Fish had been written up as a gourmet restaurant.

He parked a little way away from the restaurant. He walked towards it and looked in the windows. He saw to his dismay that the restaurant was still full. But there was Laurent, moving from table to table.

Afterwards, he was amazed at his own stupidity. Why hadn't he just waited until the restaurant had closed? Perhaps, he thought later, he was frightened that if he waited the owner might betray by nervousness that something was wrong, and it was vitally important that he be ahead of Elspeth and her television team.

Again, afterwards, he realised how lucky he was that there wasn't a television set in the restaurant or that no local had come bursting in to say they had seen the maître d' on television.

Laurent was flambéing crêpes suzette when he looked across the restaurant and saw Hamish Macbeth. He stood frozen for a moment as Hamish approached and then he threw the flaming pancakes straight at Hamish.

Hamish ducked. Diners screamed and dived under the tables. Laurent desperately threw everything he could get his hands on at Hamish: bottles of wine, plates of food, and vases of flowers. A waiter seized him and Laurent punched him in the face and sent him flying. Then he shot through the kitchen door with Hamish in pursuit.

Elspeth and her team tried to get into the restaurant but their way was blocked by escaping diners.

By dint of upsetting hot pots of food and sauce and sending them crashing down to block Hamish's way, Laurent fled out into the backyard of the restaurant. Hamish skidded in a pool of sauce and fell heavily.

He struggled to his feet, slipping and sliding and hanging on to a counter to lever himself up. "Help me catch him," he shouted to the staff who were standing, staring openmouthed.

He rushed outside into the yard. No sign of Laurent. He jumped over the wall of the yard. He looked to right and left. He should phone for backup. But he would be in deep trouble for having tried to make the arrest on his own, and he no longer had any hold over Daviot.

He shone his torch down on the ground outside the yard. There was a large muddy area but no footprints other than his own.

He turned to a waiter who had joined him.

"Is there a way into the restaurant from the yard?"

"Aye, there are steps down to the cellar."

Hamish jumped back over the wall, calling to the waiter to follow him and show him where the door was.

"You can get to the cellars from inside," said the waiter. "This end is where the stores are loaded in."

He led the way to a door. Hamish tried it. It was locked.

"Get me the key!" he shouted. The waiter ran off and came back not only with the key but with Hugo Bryan, four waiters, and Elspeth and her team.

"Stand back!" shouted Hamish. "Mr. Bryan, make

damn sure the inner door to the cellars is locked and barricade it with something."

The key was handed to Hamish. "How did Laurent lock it?" he asked.

"He's got a key," said a waiter.

Hamish's key would not work, Laurent having left his key in the lock on the other side. Hamish took a thin piece of steel out of his pocket and began to poke and fiddle in the lock until he heard the key drop down on the other side. He unlocked the door. A flight of stairs led downwards. He pressed the light switch but no light came on. Laurent had probably taken out the bulb just in case his hiding place was discovered.

The moonlight shone down into the cellar from the open door, showing boxes of stores piled up.

"Come out, Laurent!" shouted Hamish. "You can't escape now."

A can of peeled tomatoes came sailing out of the darkness with deadly accuracy and struck Hamish full on the forehead. He collapsed to his knees.

Laurent raced out of the cellar and into the full glare of a television camera. With a roar of rage, Hugo and his waiters jumped on him and bore him to the ground just as Hamish came staggering up the steps, blood streaming down his face from where the edge of the can had cut him.

Hamish wiped his face with a handkerchief and handcuffed Laurent and cautioned him.

As Hamish led Laurent out through the restaurant, he said to Hugo, who was following them, "I'm right sorry for the mess o' your restaurant."

But Hugo's eyes were shining. "Man, just think o' the publicity. My restaurant will be world-famous."

Mr. Daviot was drinking a cup of cocoa and guiltily watching his favourite programme, *Sex in the Suburbs*, when an announcer's voice broke in. "We interrupt this programme to bring you a report of the capture of the most wanted man in Britain."

And there on the screen was footage of Hamish Macbeth arresting Laurent.

Grim-faced, Daviot phoned Jimmy, who said he had known nothing about it until a moment ago when Hamish had phoned to say he had Laurent locked up in Lochdubh police station.

A convoy of police cars descended on Lochdubh. Not only was Laurent taken off for questioning but Hamish was as well.

Hamish began to wonder during the long night who the villain was as Daviot questioned him and questioned him as to why he had seen fit to go it alone.

Hamish stubbornly said that Hugo had phoned him. Before Daviot had arrived in Lochdubh, Hamish had phoned Hugo and got him to agree to saying he had phoned Hamish instead of the television station. So

Hamish said that he had to check it out because there had been so many false reports.

Why had Elspeth Grant decided that Laurent might have blacked himself up as a disguise?

"Ask her," said Hamish, who had taken the precaution of phoning Elspeth as well. "But if it hadnae been for her grand idea, we'd never have got him."

At last Hamish managed to ask if Laurent had said anything. "Not a word," said Daviot bitterly. "But we've got him for the attempted murder of you."

"Let me speak to him," begged Hamish.

Daviot was about to refuse, but he wanted everything tied up and maybe this maverick police sergeant could break Laurent's silence.

"Take Anderson with you," he said curtly.

Laurent stared at Jimmy and Hamish, his eyes gleaming with contempt in his blackened face.

After the preliminaries were over, Hamish said, "Look here, you wee scunner, at the moment the charge is the attempted murder o' me. But we are also going to charge you with torturing and killing Gaunt, the Southerns, and Liz Bentley."

"You have no proof," said Laurent.

"Circumstantial evidence," said Hamish. "Och, I'm fed up wi' this, Jimmy. How about old-fashioned police methods?"

"Meaning?" said Jimmy looking puzzled.

"Switch off the camera and tape," said Hamish

grimly. He waited until Jimmy had done so and then slammed his baton down on the table, making Laurent jump.

"Listen, wee man. I'm going to beat the hell out of you and leave no marks. Stand up!"

"You would not dare!" said Laurent.

Hamish raised his baton and sent it whistling past Laurent's head. Laurent screamed in fear.

"Missed you," said Hamish. "But how's about this?"

"I'll talk!" screamed Laurent.

Jimmy started up the tape and the video camera.

"Begin!" snapped Hamish. "Begin with Liz Bentley at Cromish."

His Quebecois accent becoming thicker in his distress, Laurent haltingly told his story.

Gaunt had wanted the drugs for himself. He had romanced Liz Bentley and had hidden them in her cottage. She had threatened to talk and so he had first tried to frighten her into silence, and when that hadn't worked, he had killed her. He still hadn't wanted to tell Dubois where the drugs were, so Dubois had advanced on him with a blowtorch and that was when Gaunt had died of a heart attack. The Southerns? They couldn't talk because Gaunt hadn't told them where the drugs were and so Dubois had tortured them and killed them.

It had all started as Hamish had guessed. The Canadian police had got wind of a large drug haul which had made its way to Canada from Colombia. They did not know about Dubois, a shadowy figure in the crime world. He had immediately searched around for a way to get the drugs out of the country. Southern had heard about the haul and put out feelers to say he knew how to get the drugs out of the country. He would hire a large fishing vessel in Newfoundland to take them off with the drugs; Gaunt would arrange for a small boat to meet the vessel at sea and take the drugs to safety. He would hide them and then contact Dubois—which he had failed to do. So Dubois, Laurent, and Xavier had gone in search of them.

Laurent knew nothing about the diamond rings, one found in Liz's shed and the other at the schoolhouse. Hamish could only guess it was some way of them identifying each other.

"I'll have you for assault," said Laurent, and then he began to cry.

"Did you see me assault him?" Hamish asked Jimmy.

"Not me," said Jimmy. "Let's leave this wee bastard to cool for a bit."

Epilogue

☠

Nine fathom deep he had followed us
From the land of mist and snow.

—Coleridge

Reports in triplicate. Reports piled on reports. Long interviews with every customer who had been in the restaurant when Laurent was arrested, along with interviews with all the staff. Then all those had to be typed out by Hamish and sent to Strathbane.

He was called up before several committees of hard-eyed men headed by Chief Superintendent Douglas to explain his odd behaviour in deciding to go to Golspie on his own. One waspish little man whose rank Hamish did not know was vehement in claiming that Hamish was a publicity seeker who had made sure a television team would be there at the restaurant.

At the end of it all, he felt he had saved his police station by a whisker and all thanks to Daviot, who had stuck to his word that the Lochdubh police station would be safe. But there was one last question. Why was there no report about those diamond rings: no report about searching jewellers throughout Scotland to see who had commissioned the rings?

Hamish said patiently that he had assumed that the special force or Strathbane would have covered that. Jimmy Anderson was sent for.

He said he had sent out a description of the rings to every jeweller in the United Kingdom but had not met with any success, so he supposed the rings had been made by some crooked jeweller somewhere or other. "It's all in my report," he said impatiently.

"There is no such report on the files," retorted Douglas.

"I gave my report to Chief Detective Inspector Blair," said Jimmy.

Blair was summoned. He furiously denied that he had received such a report. "I still have it on my computer along with a report of the date I gave it to you," said Jimmy. "I'll get it now."

"Leave us and take Macbeth with you," said Douglas. "No, Mr. Blair, you stay."

"Blair's toast," said Jimmy cheerfully as he and Hamish walked down the stairs together. "Say hullo to your new boss. Me!"

"Don't bet on it," said Hamish gloomily. "Daviot will be doing his best to hang on to his creature."

*   *   *

And that was exactly what Daviot was doing. Wanting to avoid promotion and so be transferred to Strathbane, Hamish had let Blair take the credit for a number of crimes that he himself had solved. So Daviot was reading out a list of Blair's "successes" while Blair sat with his eyes lowered, the very picture of modesty.

Apart from learning that Laurent really was his first name and his second name was Dejeux, and apart from the fact that Laurent was to stand trial in Edinburgh, Hamish heard no more about the case. The paperwork was finished and there were new and exciting news stories to take the press away.

It was as if it all suddenly went quiet. Christine Dalray phoned to invite Hamish to dinner but he put her off because a good part of him hankered after Anka. The scar on his forehead where he had been struck by that tin of tomatoes had healed up, and his fiery hair had grown back in over the old wound.

He was just thinking about going to Braikie to see if he could persuade the elusive Anka to go on a date with him when the phone rang. It was Dr. Williams. "Can you get up here?" he pleaded. "She's gone mad!"

"What happened?"

"I tried to shoot that fox."

"Oh, my," said Hamish. "I'll be there right away."

As he drove north, his thoughts turned to Elspeth. He knew she would have been firmly instructed to keep clear of him by Strathbane. He knew he was forbidden from making any statements to the media, but he thought she might at least have called to see how he was.

It was a grey, misty day. No colour in the landscape. He drove on until Cromish came into view through the mist like a sort of Brigadoon.

A little huddle of curious villagers was standing outside Samantha's cottage. Screams and cries were coming from inside. The door was open. Hamish walked in.

Samantha was sitting at the kitchen table. Dr. Williams was backed against the kitchen dresser, looking helpless. Broken crockery lay scattered over the floor. Between sobs, Samantha threw back her head and let out an eldritch scream.

Hamish gave her a firm slap on the face. She stared at him in shock. He handed her a clean handkerchief and said, "Behave yourself!"

He turned to Dr. Williams. "What exactly happened?"

"We were sleeping at my place last night. The mist hadn't come down and you know it never really gets that dark this time o' year. I woke up and she was standing by the window. I asked what was up. She said, 'Oh, it's Foxy. Come and look.' I went and got my shotgun and went out into the garden. It was a great dog fox. I took aim but she jerked my arm up.

Then she went into hysterics and fled the house in her nightie. She let me in this morning, screaming I was a murderer, throwing plates at me along with her engagement ring."

"Go and get your bag and give her a sedative. Hurry!"

Hamish sat down next to Samantha and put an arm round her shoulder. "I thought you had come to your senses about foxes," he said.

She gulped and gave a choked sob. "I'd heard about the seer in Lochdubh."

"Aye. Angus Macdonald. Go on."

"It was weird. I told him about how silly I had been about that fox. I really wanted my fortune told. He closed his eyes and he said in a faraway voice that Foxy was actually the soul of someone who had come back and should be treated with respect. I did not tell Harold but I decided to protect that fox with my life if necessary."

What the hell was Angus playing at? Hamish was determined to see him as soon as possible.

"I cannot live amongst such savagery," said Samantha. "I am going back to Edinburgh."

"Good idea," said Hamish, thinking that Dr. Williams was well out of it.

When the doctor returned, Hamish coaxed Samantha into swallowing a sedative and together they got her into bed.

They retreated to the kitchen. "Man, the woman's unbalanced," said Hamish. "And you a doctor."

Dr. Williams shrugged. "The sex was good. But I can't have anything to do with her after this."

"The trouble was caused when the seer in Lochdubh told her that fox was the soul of someone who had come back. I'm going to see him and find out what he was up to. Let's get out of here."

When they walked out to where the villagers were waiting, to Hamish's alarm Dr. Williams told them what the seer had said and that it had turned Samantha's mind.

Hamish pulled the doctor away and when they were clear of the crowd, he whispered fiercely, "You've got Mr. Foxy for life. Not one o' that superstitious lot are going to touch the beast now."

Once in Lochdubh, Hamish went straight to see Angus Macdonald. "No, I havenae brought ye a present, you auld fraud," roared Hamish.

"Come in and calm down," said Angus. "I see a fox in your eyes."

"And I feel like blacking yours," said Hamish. "What possessed you to tell Samantha Trent that the fox was the soul of someone who had come back?"

"Well, I ken it's like this. I have this niece in Lochinver, Bella Macdonald, my late brother's daughter. She's a widow. She met Dr. Williams at a concert in Lochinver and really fancied him. They went out for a bit and all was looking hopeful when he got snared by the fox lady. Now, with her out o' the road, my Bella stands a good chance."

"I'm going to tell Williams what you did," said Hamish.

"So you would want to see a grand man like Dr. Williams shackled to a nutcase?"

"No, but you nearly caused Samantha Trent to have a heart attack. You're a wicked, interfering old scunner!"

"Great, isn't it? Now push off, Hamish."

Hamish wrestled with his conscience and finally phoned Dr. Williams. "How is she?" he asked.

"Woke up a bit ago. But she's packing up. She's determined to get back to Edinburgh. Why did that seer tell her such a load of rubbish?"

"Because he thinks you'd be better off with his niece, Bella Macdonald."

"I remember her. Nice lady, but she's got a bit of a moustache."

"She can shave, dammit!" said Hamish, suddenly fed up with the whole business.

That night, the old dog fox roused himself to go hunting. He was tired and hungry. His family had been trapped and killed long ago. He sniffed the air. He slunk down to the nearest garden, where he could smell roast chicken. To his amazement, a whole roast chicken was on a plate near the hedge. He gobbled it up. Now there was the scent of beef in the air. In the next garden, he found a slice of steak.

And so it went on. Each superstitious villager was convinced the old fox held the soul of a lost loved one.

When he was found dead six months later, the villagers gave the old fox a Christian burial, even having a coffin constructed, which had to be quite large for a fox as the animal was very fat indeed.

Hamish, finding his life was tranquil once more—and because it was Sunday and he knew the bakery would be closed—went to Braikie to pay a call on Dick and Anka.

Dick gave him an enthusiastic welcome. Because he had lost weight with all the work in the bakery he did not look at all like the old Dick, but Anka was breathtakingly beautiful as usual.

When Dick had gone through to the kitchen to fetch coffee and cakes, Hamish asked Anka if she would have dinner with him one evening.

"I don't think so," said Anka. "Apart from Sunday, I do not have any free time. Maybe later, when we hire more staff."

Hamish brightened. She hadn't said no. But when

Dick came back with a laden tray, Anka said, "Hamish has said he will take us out for dinner one evening."

"That's great," said Dick. "We'll let you know."

We, thought Hamish sulkily on the road home. His pets were in the passenger seat beside him. Sonsie put a large paw on Hamish's knee.

"Aye, you're a grand cat," said Hamish, "but no substitute for a nice lassie."

His thoughts turned to Christine Dalray. Hugo Bryan had promised Hamish a free meal for himself and a friend anytime he cared to come over to the restaurant.

At the station, Hamish phoned Christine, but she said she was busy.

He went out to the waterfront, followed by his animals. Archie Maclean came to join him. "Do you understand women, Archie?" asked Hamish.

Archie jerked his hand towards his cottage, from which came the sounds of ferocious cleaning. "Me? Havenae a clue," he said.

Hamish looked down at Archie's tight tweed suit. "I thought your missus had stopped boiling your clothes and making you wear tight stuff."

"Herself boils everything," said Archie. "Do you need a bit o' sex?"

"Don't we all?"

"I'll gie ye the address o' this wumman over at Lairg. She's no' expensive."

"Archie! I'm amazed. A prostitute."

"Och, no. Just a nice widow woman who earns a bit on the side. I'd better get indoors. Here's Angela."

Angela Brodie came up to join Hamish. "Does life seem dull after all that excitement?"

"How's your man?"

"He's away at a medical conference in Edinburgh."

"Tell you what," said Hamish. "I've been offered a free meal at thon restaurant in Golspie. Care to come with me tonight?"

"Oh, I'd like that."

"I'll pick you up at seven o'clock this evening."

And at seven that evening, Nessie Currie twitched the net curtains on her front window which overlooked the waterfront and let out an exclamation of surprise. She was joined by her sister, Jessie.

Hamish Macbeth in his best suit was getting into Amanda Brodie's car. Nessie, as usual, thought the worst. "The doctor's away. Macbeth is at it again with his philandering ways."

She was so upset, she ignored her sister's usual chorus of her last words.

"He must be stopped," she said firmly. "He'll be taking her somewhere for dinner and plying her wi' wine."

With a research diligence worthy of Hamish Macbeth, Nessie sat down by the phone and began to contact every restaurant she could think of, at last finding the right one.

Grimly, the sisters put on their coats and hats and set out for Golspie.

Christine and her partner for the evening had a table at the restaurant window. Her partner was a small, clever man called Phil Murchison from the DNA lab in Glasgow. He was in his forties with the disadvantages of a large nose and a gleaming bald head. But he was amusing and witty.

Christine saw Hamish Macbeth arriving outside and gave an exclamation. "What is it?" asked Phil.

"It's that police sergeant, Hamish Macbeth. He's standing out there with a clothes brush, brushing some woman down."

Angela was wearing a black trouser suit. Hamish had pointed out it was covered in cat hairs from Angela's many cats. Angela had found a clothes brush in the backseat and had told him to get rid of the hairs before they went into the restaurant.

"You'll do now," said Hamish. "Come along. I'm hungry."

The first person Hamish saw when he entered the restaurant was Christine. He nodded to her and would have walked past but Phil jumped to his feet and cried, "Hamish Macbeth! I've heard so much about you."

Hamish introduced Angela, and Christine introduced Phil. No competition there, thought Christine, surveying Angela's wispy hair and vague face.

The owner came hurrying up. "Do you all want to sit together?" he asked.

"No," began Hamish, but Phil said, "Would you mind, Hamish? I want to hear all about your adventures."

"All right," said Hamish, wondering how he could possibly have forgotten that Christine was so attractive.

They were all ushered to a table for four. A waiter came hurrying up with a bottle of champagne. "Compliments of the management," he said.

"We'd only arrived a few minutes before you," said Christine. "We'll talk after we order, yes?"

Hamish leaned forward and whispered to Angela, "Remember, I'm not paying for this, so order anything you want."

Angela smiled up at him. That smile of Angela's transformed her face.

Hamish had thought nouvelle cuisine with all its decorated pawky portions had gone out of fashion. Angela had ordered scallops but only got two decorated with rocket. Hamish's venison pâté was a small cube with a sliver of toast. Christine and Phil had both ordered prawns Marie Rose, which came in small metal bowls of the kind that used to be used in ice cream parlours. Angela said to Hamish that she would confine herself to one glass of champagne, as she was driving.

Phil and Hamish were soon deep in conversation. "Have you known Hamish long?" asked Christine.

"Yes. I live in Lochdubh," said Angela.

"And do you and Hamish often go out together?"

"Sometimes. When my husband is away, of course," said Angela innocently.

So the rumours of Hamish being a philanderer were true, thought Christine. Thank goodness she had never taken him all that seriously.

Christine could sense a closeness between Angela and Hamish, not knowing that closeness was caused by friendship.

The door opened and the Currie sisters walked in, the candlelight shining on their thick glasses.

At first, they looked taken back to see Christine and Phil as well as Hamish and Angela. But Nessie knew where her duty lay.

"You should be ashamed of yourself, Mrs. Brodie," she said in a loud voice.

"Ashamed. Brodie," chorused her sister.

"I am simply trying to enjoy a dinner with Hamish and his friends," said Angela.

"'As water spilt upon the ground, that cannot be gathered up,' so it is with your reputation," said Nessie.

"Reputation," intoned Jessie.

Hamish took out his phone and called Dr. Brodie on

his mobile. "Talk some sense into the Currie sisters," he said. "They've just arrived in the restaurant to accuse poor Angela of having an affair with me."

"Oh, let me speak to them," said Dr. Brodie.

Hamish handed the phone to Nessie. Hamish heard her exclaim, "You knew?"

When Nessie finally rang off, Hamish said severely, "I think the pair of you should go home and scrub your brains out with soap."

But Nessie was not to be defeated. "I've heard of wife swapping," she said, "but what's worse, Macbeth, is you haven't even got a wife to swap."

"Outside!" ordered Hamish, and thrusting them before him, he got them out of the restaurant.

"You'll be hearing from my lawyer," he said to Nessie.

Nessie quailed. She knew she had gone too far.

"I felt it was my Christian duty to save Mrs. Brodie's reputation."

Hamish ignored her sister's bleating chorus. "The only people damaging Angela's reputation and mine are you and your sister."

"No lawyer," said Nessie in a frightened voice. "We'll go back in and apologise."

"*No!* Chust go away!"

When Hamish went back in and sat down, Phil said, "And here's me thinking that life in a highland village would be quiet and peaceful. But it's all murder and mayhem and madwomen." He turned to Angela. "How does it feel to be a scarlet woman?"

"It's rather fun," said Angela. "But surely you have a lot of excitement in a big city like Aberdeen."

Phil began to tell several very amusing stories. Hamish had ordered fillet of sea bass. He got what he estimated to be half a fillet, three boiled potatoes decorated with parsley, and half a tomato.

"Excuse me," he said. He picked up his plate and went into the kitchen where Hugo was sitting at a table in the corner. "Look at this wee bittie o' fish," said Hamish. "Are you trying to starve me?"

"It's the new chef. He says folk like artistic food."

"I didnae see any locals in the dining room," said Hamish. "Come the winter, you'll find you'll get few customers unless you feed them. I know I shouldnae complain, seeing as I'm not paying, but you do need some advice."

Hamish returned to the table and moodily ate his fish.

But Hugo had taken Hamish's words to heart. The cheese board when it appeared was enormous. There was a presentation bottle of port.

"I hate to sound like a policeman," said Hamish. "But are you and Christine going to drive?"

"No, we booked rooms at the local hotel. We can walk along."

Hearing that Angela was a writer, Phil began to question her about her books.

Hamish turned to Christine. "I gather there's been no sign of Dubois's body?"

"No. They searched and searched. But the coast-guard people say that the currents off those cliffs are so strong, the body could be halfway to America by now."

Hamish felt happy and slightly tipsy on the road home. For the first time since Dick had left, he really began to relish the idea of having his station all to himself.

He got out of Angela's car and strolled towards the police station. Then he stopped and frowned. His usual parking place at the side of the restaurant was blocked by a large, dusty Jeep Cherokee. He approached cautiously, wishing he were in uniform and had his belt with the stun gun on it with him.

He looked in the driver's window. A giant of a fair-haired policeman was asleep at the wheel.

Hamish rapped on the window. The policeman started awake, opened the car door, and got out. Hamish was six feet, five inches in height. He estimated this giant topped him by a couple of inches.

He beamed at Hamish. "Charlie Carter, sir."

"What's happened?" asked Hamish.

"Didn't they tell you? I'm your new policeman."

"No, they didn't," said Hamish. "You'd best come in until we discuss it."

In the light of the kitchen, Charlie was revealed as having broad shoulders and very large hands and feet. He had a big head, thick fair hair, and bright-blue eyes in a square pleasant face.

"Sit down," said Hamish, feeling crowded. Charlie sat down, and the chair creaked under his weight. The flap on the kitchen door opened and Sonsie and Lugs slouched in. To Hamish's surprise, they paid no attention to the newcomer. A wild cat and a dog with large ears and blue eyes made a strange pair, but Charlie did not seem to find them odd.

"So," said Hamish, sitting down opposite Charlie, "how long have you been in the force?"

"A week," said Charlie. "I left the Scottish Police College and got a posting to Strathbane." His voice had the soft fluting tones of the Outer Hebrides.

"Do you know why they sent you here?"

"They said you were in need of a policeman," said Charlie.

"Dick Fraser, the policeman who was here before, left his bed and some furnishings, but I doubt if the bed will be big enough for you."

"I'm good at the carpentry," said Charlie. "I'm sure I can fix something."

"Well, bring your things in and we'll see you settled."

Charlie stood up and snagged his head against the overhanging lightbulb, knocking it out of its shade and plunging the kitchen into darkness.

"Oh, I'm sorry." He trod on Hamish's toes and Hamish let out a yelp of pain. "Go away!" said Hamish. "I'll fix the light."

When Charlie eventually went to bed for the night, Hamish stood outside the police station and phoned Jimmy. "Whassamatter?" demanded Jimmy. "You woke me up."

"Tell me about Charlie Carter."

Jimmy began to laugh. "Clumsy Charlie. He tipped a cup of hot coffee into Blair's lap, he tripped over his large feet and crashed into one of the computers and broke it, a drawer on one of the old filing cabinets was stuck and he jerked it open so hard that the whole cabinet fell on him, he…"

"Enough," said Hamish. "I'll figure out a way to get rid of him."

"Mind you," said Jimmy, "he graduated police college at the top o' the class."

But the next day found Hamish warming to the large policeman. He was so good-natured. His clumsiness did not extend to animals and he deftly helped Hamish dip his sheep. Sonsie and Lugs seemed to adore him.

Hamish then took him round the village and introduced him to various people. At one point, Charlie paused and looked over the shining sea loch and then

DEATH OF A LIAR 261

at the row of whitewashed cottages along the waterfront.

"This is paradise," he said.

He'll do, thought Hamish happily.

But something happened that made him decide the
tall policeman had to go.

The following day, he told Charlie to look after the
station because he was going up to Cromish to find out
if Samantha was all right.

Charlie said the front garden needed a bit of weed-
ing and he would pass the time doing that.

Shortly after Hamish had left, he heard a female
voice outside shouting, "Anybody home?"

He lumbered round to the kitchen door and stood
there with his mouth open looking down at Priscilla.

"Have I a spot on my nose or something?" demanded Priscilla.

"Oh, no," breathed Charlie. "I've never seen a lady
as beautiful as you off the television."

Priscilla smiled up at Charlie. "I came to see Hamish."

"He's gone up to Cromish."

"I was going to take him to lunch." Charlie was
standing holding a trowel. He was not in uniform.

"Never tell me Hamish has employed a gardener,"
said Priscilla.

"No. I'm his new policeman."

"Well, welcome to Lochdubh. I tell you what, I'll
take you to lunch instead."

"I'll just give myself a wash and be with you," said Charlie happily.

In the Italian restaurant, Charlie pulled out Priscilla's chair as she was about to sit down. Unfortunately, he pulled it out too far and she fell on the floor. He picked Priscilla up in his arms, hooked the chair upright, and sat her down.

He sat down opposite, his face flaming. "I'm right sorry." He waved his arms and sent the water jug crashing onto the floor.

More flustered apologies and a lecture from waiter Willie Lamont.

Priscilla thought Charlie as like a big child. She asked him questions about his family. He said his father was a crofter in Lewis and that his mother was dead. He had no brothers or sisters. All the time, he gazed at Priscilla with such open admiration that she began to feel he was the nicest man she had met in ages.

She asked him how he was settling in at the police station and he said it was fine but that he would have to get to work on the bed because it was too small.

"I seem to remember," said Priscilla, "that we have a long single bed down in one of the storerooms at the hotel. If it's still there, you can have it."

Willie Lamont uneasily watched the couple. He went back into the kitchen and said to his wife, Lucia,

"I should phone Hamish. Thon new copper's a right canosovas."

"A Casanova, you mean," said Lucia. "Leave them alone."

By the time the meal was over and the bed had been found for Charlie and delivered to the police station, Priscilla and Charlie were firm friends.

In Cromish, Hamish found Samantha's cottage was empty; there was a FOR SALE board outside. He called on Dr. Williams.

"She left yesterday," said the doctor. "I should have known the woman wasn't right in the head. But she seduced me and I'd been celibate a long time. You know how it is."

"I do indeed," said Hamish bitterly. "Have you contacted the seer's niece?"

"Not yet. Maybe not. I don't like being manipulated. How are things with you?"

"I've been given a new policeman. He's a clumsy sort of giant but he's kind and a hard worker. Makes a change from Dick Fraser, my former copper. I hope this one doesn't desert me for food. My first policeman married the daughter of a restaurant owner and now waits table, the second is chef at the Tommel Castle Hotel, and the last one, Dick Fraser who you met, is running a bakery in Braikie."

"Does the latest one show any signs of liking to cook?"

"No, I'm back to cooking the meals. I'll drop by the shop and get some baps to take back with me."

"Next time you see Angus Macdonald, tell him from me that he's a bastard."

"Will do."

When Hamish returned in the afternoon, he heard hammering coming from the back of the police station and went to look at what was happening.

"I'm just dismantling this bed," said Charlie. "Priscilla gave me a new one."

"How did you meet Priscilla?"

"She came to ask you to lunch but took me instead," said Charlie. "What a beauty! Then she took me up to the hotel and got me this nice long bed out of storage."

From that moment, it seemed to poor Charlie that the normally amiable Hamish had taken a dislike to him. Nerves made him clumsier than ever.

The next morning, Hamish gave him a list of places to visit on the extensive beat of Sutherland, and when Charlie had driven off, Hamish went up to the Tommel Castle Hotel.

Priscilla was in the gift shop, helping the assistant open boxes of newly arrived goods. She smiled at Hamish and said, "Come over to the hotel. I could do with a coffee."

Once they were seated in a corner of the hotel lounge, Priscilla immediately began to sing Charlie's praises. "You're so lucky, Hamish, to have such a good-natured sidekick."

"He's too clumsy, Priscilla. He'll have to go."

"Oh, Hamish. That would be so cruel. He loves it here."

"I don't love him here. The police station is not big enough to have an ox like Charlie blundering about."

"Not jealous, are you?"

That unfortunate streak of highland malice in Hamish's character reared its ugly head.

"What on earth is there to be jealous about?" he said nastily. "It's not as if I have any interest in you."

"A man like Charlie," said Priscilla in a thin voice, "has the knack of making a woman feel admired and cherished, something you are never able to do."

"Pah!" said Hamish. "He's going."

As if to suit the black mood in the police station that night, a storm had risen. It shrieked round the station as Hamish told Charlie he was getting rid of him.

Charlie simply bowed his large head and said nothing. The cat crawled up onto his lap, and he stroked her soft fur.

Hamish woke the following morning. The wind was still blowing in great squally, tearing gusts. At first he thought he had a hangover and slowly realised he felt sick with guilt.

He decided to go up to the cliffs where Dubois had tried to kill him. He had often gone there in the past when he felt he needed the tumult of wind and waves to clear his brain. He ordered his pets to stay, walked past Charlie who was sitting at the kitchen table, and went out into the storm.

Charlie sat with his large hands clutched round a mug of coffee. He suddenly decided to follow Hamish and see if he could make Hamish change his mind.

It was as if the whole countryside was in motion. It whistled through the ruins of the old hotel at the entrance to the harbour. It sent whitecapped waves racing down the loch as if they were trying to flee the Atlantic breakers beyond the cliffs.

Ragged black clouds tore across the sky above, and as Hamish approached the cliffs, he could hear the clamour of the ocean. The wind was too strong even for the gulls, who were no doubt sheltering on their ledges, and the puffins were down in their burrows.

Hamish took the steep path leading up to the top of the cliffs. Several times the wind almost blew him over. As on the night when he had nearly been killed, great waves were rising up above the cliffs. He remembered the horrible scene. It was suddenly infinitely precious to him that his police station was secure and that the village of Lochdubh had returned to its normal placid existence.

One great wave rose high above the cliff and crashed down over the top. Seawater flowed down over the heather. Apart from the night Dubois was swept away, Hamish had never seen such a huge wave. He squinted at his watch. High tide was nearly over.

He was unaware that Charlie was standing some paces behind him, trying to summon up courage to speak to him.

Hamish was about to turn away when another giant wave rose above the cliffs. He stood mesmcrised. It hurtled a great object at his feet and then drew back through the heather with a hissing sound.

Hamish looked down and clutched his hair. Lying at his feet was what remained of the body of Dubois, barely recognisable. The gaseous body has been torn by the rocks and the eyes eaten by sea creatures. Two empty sockets stared up at him.

"Is that Dubois?" said Charlie, coming up to stand beside him.

"That," shouted Hamish, "is weeks o' paperwork and interrogations and more paperwork. Why couldn't the man stay lost?"

Charlie looked at Hamish. He looked down at the body.

With one swift movement, he bent down and picked up the carcase and ran to the top of the cliffs.

"Come back!" yelled Hamish. "You'll get washed away."

But before the next wave rose up, Charlie hurled the body over the cliffs.

He came back to join Hamish. "I don't think you need to bother about paperwork now, sir."

Hamish looked at Charlie in open admiration. "Come to the pub and I'll get us a drink."

Outside the pub, a wheelie bin came racing along. Charlie caught it, took off his oilskin, stuffed it inside, and threw the bin in the loch.

"Smelled o' dead body," said Charlie.

They went into the pub. "It may be early for a dram, but I need one," said Hamish.

"Me, too," said Charlie.

"Get that table by the window and I'll get the drinks," said Hamish.

He returned with two double whiskies and sat down opposite Charlie.

"I owe you an apology, Charlie," said Hamish. "I was that jealous o' you."

"Me?" said Charlie amazed. "No one's ever jealous o' me."

"I used to be engaged to Priscilla," said Hamish.

"Oh, dear. Why did she call it off?"

"It just didnae work out," said Hamish, "but when I heard her singing your praises, well, I got nasty and spiteful. Of course you can stay."

"No one told me about Priscilla," said Charlie. "When I was out on the beat, some folk said they thought you might be going to marry that television presenter, Elspeth Grant."

"I have no luck with the ladies."

"Don't worry about me, sir. Priscilla is just friendly-like. She doesn't fancy me one bit."

"The storm's dying down," said Hamish. "Thanks for getting rid of that body."

Charlie grinned. "What body? I never saw any body at all."

They went back to the police station together and then set off in the Land Rover to call round places on their beat and make sure the old people in particular had not had their properties damaged by the storm.

When they returned to the station, Hamish found he had a message from Christine. "This is my last invitation to dinner, Hamish. Phone me if you're free."

Why not, thought Hamish. He phoned her back and arranged to meet her in a restaurant in Strathbane the following evening.

He suddenly remembered Heather Green down in Beauly and wondered how she was getting on. He told Charlie about her and suggested that the next morning they should go down to Beauly and see how she was coping with life.

But when they called at her home, a stranger answered the door. He said he had recently bought the house and that Heather Green, he believed, was living in sheltered housing at the far end of the village.

Hamish felt depressed. He was sure Heather would be grieving for her lost home. They found out where she was living and knocked at the door of her flat.

A healthier-looking Heather answered the door, smiled at them, and ushered them in. It was a very small flat, but warm and comfortable.

"I'm sorry you had to sell your home," said Hamish.

"Oh, I was so silly about that. A friend took me to show me these places. There's even a warden to do my shopping if I want. I got an awful lot of money for the house and so I'm well set up. Now, I'll make tea and then you must tell me of your adventures. I not only have the television now but a phone as well!"

When they left an hour later, Hamish had a feeling of being at peace with the world.

When they returned to the police station, they found Jimmy waiting for them.

"You remember Barney Mailer?"

Hamish searched his memory. "I have it. The chap who was supposed to have been romancing Liz and moved to London?"

"That's the one. We couldnae seem to find him but it turned out he had moved to Thailand. He contacted us and we spoke to him on the phone. He said she showed him that ring and said she was a member of a gang and that was the way they recognised each other. He thought she was mad so he cleared off."

"Such a childish thing to do," said Hamish, "but probably Gaunt had some of them try to con people out of their money. Tell me, Jimmy," he went on, "why does Daviot keep that horror Blair in his job?"

"You know why. Blair creeps and cringes. Daviot's a weak man. I sometimes think of getting a transfer."

"Don't do that!" said Hamish alarmed. "If you went, I'd never learn anything at all. This is the first time you haven't asked for whisky."

"Got a stiff warning from the doctor. But man, it's hard."

The following evening, Hamish, dressed in his best, set out for Strathbane. As soon as he had gone, Charlie drove up to the hotel to see Priscilla.

Christine's choice of restaurant was a steak house. In the soft light of the restaurant, she looked more attractive than ever. As they talked shop, Hamish covertly studied her and wondered if one really needed to be in love to get married. Folk said passion didn't last. It was compatibility and friendship that mattered in the long run.

Christine had said he could stay the night in her flat and so they shared a bottle of wine.

I'll do it, thought Hamish. I'll ask her to marry me.

"There you are!" cried a female voice. A tall woman was smiling down at them.

"Fiona!" cried Christine. "Hamish, this is my sister. Fiona, Hamish Macbeth. Join us. When did you arrive? I didn't expect you until Saturday."

"Came earlier, that's all."

"Hamish, you'll need to sleep on the sofa. My sister is staying with me," said Christine.

The two women plunged into family reminiscences. Hamish suddenly wanted to leave. What madness had possessed him to even think of proposing to Christine?

Fiona suddenly turned her attention to Hamish and demanded to be told all about murders.

"Excuse me," said Hamish. "Back in a minute."

He went to the loo and phoned Jimmy. "Don't ask," he said. "Phone me in five minutes' time and tell me I'm wanted at headquarters."

He returned to the table. He knew immediately he had been discussed. Fiona gave him a sly look. "How long have you and my sister been…er…friends?"

"We've worked on a few cases," said Hamish.

His mobile rang. He answered it, listened, and rang off.

"That was Jimmy, Christine. I've got to go to headquarters."

"I'll come with you."

"No, I'll phone if it's anything important. I'll pay for this on the road out."

*   *   *

Hoping he wouldn't be stopped and breathalysed, Hamish drove slowly to Lochdubh.

He felt all the strains of the murder cases and the attacks on his life fading away.

He was going home, and he was suddenly happy again at last.

About the Author

M. C. Beaton has won international acclaim for her bestselling Hamish Macbeth mysteries, and the BBC has aired twenty-four episodes based on the series. Also the author of the Agatha Raisin series, M. C. Beaton lives in a Cotswold cottage with her husband. For more information, you can visit www.MCBeaton.com.

SAVOR THE FLAVORS OF SCOTLAND

WITH ANOTHER HAMISH MACBETH MYSTERY BY M. C. BEATON!

Please see the next page
for a preview of

Death of a Nurse.

Available now.

Chapter One

☠

I wish I loved the Human Race;
I wish I loved its silly face;
I wish I liked the way it walks;
I wish I liked the way it talks:
And when I'm introduced to one
I wish I thought What Jolly Fun!

—Sir Walter A. Raleigh

Police Sergeant Hamish Macbeth was in a sour mood, despite the sunny, windy weather. His new sidekick, policeman Charlie Carter, was giving him claustrophobia. Admittedly Charlie was kind and amiable and worked hard. But he was big, very big. Hamish was tall but Charlie was taller and broader, and he was clumsy. He fell over the furniture, he broke china and glass, and when Hamish shouted at him, he looked so miserable that Hamish immediately felt guilty.

Hamish's odd-looking dog called Lugs walked at his heels as did his wild cat, Sonsie. Wild cats are an endangered species and Hamish was always afraid that Sonsie would be taken away. As if sensing his master's bad mood, Lugs looked up at Hamish with his strange blue eyes.

The breeze sent sunny ripples dancing across the sea loch. The village of Lochdubh in Sutherland looked like a picture postcard with its row of small eighteenth-century whitewashed cottages facing the sea loch. Hamish was leaning on the seawall, thinking dark thoughts about getting Charlie transferred back to Strathbane, that ghastly town full of drugs and crime.

He turned away from the wall, and that was when he saw a vision. A nurse came tripping along with a shopping basket over her arm. From her jaunty cap to her candy-striped dress and her black stockings, she looked like a fantasy nurse. She went into Patel's grocery store and Hamish followed. He waited outside until she emerged with a basket full of groceries over her arm. He swept off his cap. "May I carry your messages for you?"

She smiled up at him from a perfect oval of a face. Her large eyes were grey and fringed with heavy lashes. Her hair, under the cap, was fair and glossy.

"Thank you," she said. "But my car is right there."

"I'll put them in the boot for you," said Hamish. "Do you work near here?"

"Yes, I am a private nurse. I take care of old Mr. Harrison."

"He lives in that old hunting lodge out on the Braikie road," said Hamish. "But he had a nurse, a Miss Macduff."

She laughed. "He fired her and employed me. So you're the local copper."

"Hamish Macbeth. And you are?"

"Gloria Dainty."

He put her basket in the boot. She bent over the boot to arrange something and the frisky wind lifted the skirt of her dress, revealing that those stockings were held up with lacy suspenders.

"I'll follow you," said Hamish. "I haven't said hullo to Mr. Harrison." He had actually visited the old man, ignoring the fact that Mr. Harrison had said sourly that he did not want visitors. But he was determined to further his acquaintance with Gloria.

Charlie Carter knew in his bones that Hamish wanted rid of him. He could not bear the idea of leaving Lochdubh. He was trying to make a cup of tea without breaking or spilling anything when there was a knock at the door. When he opened it, he found Priscilla Halburton-Smythe smiling at him.

"I'm afraid Hamish is out," said Charlie. "I'm about to make tea. Like some?"

"Yes, please." Priscilla sat down at the kitchen table. Various pieces of china, recently mended, stood on a piece of newspaper. "Have you been breaking much?" she asked sympathetically.

"Hamish gets so mad at me," said Charlie. "And that makes me worse. Fact is, it is a wee station and we're two big men." He poured tea carefully and then sat down gingerly opposite her. Even sitting down, his head was near the low ceiling. The kitchen chair creaked alarmingly under his weight. His normally pleasant face looked so miserable that Priscilla was touched. Because of her beauty, until Charlie came along, Priscilla had never been able to have a male friend.

"I've just remembered something," she said. "In the basement at the castle, there's a little apartment which used to be the butler's place before we turned it into a hotel. It has high ceilings."

Charlie brightened and then his face fell. "I'm supposed to live in police accommodation."

"Nobody would know, apart from me and Hamish. Oh, maybe the villagers, but they won't talk. Let's go now and have a look."

Hamish, as he followed Gloria into the dark hall of the hunting lodge, remembered again that Mr. Harrison was a nasty old man who had sneered at him when Hamish had visited. He carried the shopping basket into a cavernous kitchen. "Just put the basket on the table," said Gloria, "and come through to the drawing room and say hullo."

"Isn't there a housekeeper to do the shopping?" asked Hamish.

"Yes, but this stuff is for me. Mr. Harrison has a Latvian couple to look after him, Juris and Inga Janson. I prefer to cook my own food. Must look after my figure."

Oh, let *me* look after it for you, thought Hamish dreamily.

"Come along," she said briskly.

As he followed her through a dark stone-flagged passage and across the shadowy hall where only weak light filtered through the mullioned windows, Hamish reflected that the hunting box had probably been built at the end of the nineteenth century when there was a craze for Gothic architecture. Stuffed animals' heads looked down from the thick stone walls. A stone staircase with a stone banister led upwards.

Gloria pushed open a heavy oak door, stood aside, and called, "Here is our local bobby to see you, Mr. Harrison."

An old man with his knees covered in a tartan rug was seated in a wheelchair by a French window overlooking a terrace where a few dead leaves skittered along in the breeze.

He swung his chair round. "He's already said hullo. Where the hell are the Jansons? I want a drink."

"I'll get it," said Gloria. "Your usual whisky and soda? What about you, Hamish?"

"Too early for me," said Hamish.

"Sanctimonious prick," commented Mr. Harrison.

He had a thick head of hair and bushy eyebrows. His eyes were small and black.

"You see this copper here, Gloria?" he demanded. "This is just the sort of chap you want to avoid. If he had any guts or ambition, he would have risen in the ranks instead of being stuck in the back of nowhere."

"Like you," said Hamish.

"Here's your drink, my dear," said Gloria soothingly. "Aren't we a bit cross this morning?"

Mr. Harrison took the glass from her and his face softened. "What would I do without you? Push off, copper."

Hamish smiled. "If you ever need my help, forget it."

"I'll see you out," said Gloria.

Hamish hesitated at the front door. "Any chance of taking you out for dinner one evening? There's a very good restaurant in Lochdubh."

"I'm allowed a day off a week. Every Sunday. Maybe that would be nice."

"What about next Sunday? I'll drive so you can have a drink."

"If Mr. Harrison saw you, I don't think he would approve. I'll get Juris to run me there. What time?"

"Say eight o'clock?"

"Fine."

"You're not going to bring those creepy animals with you, are you?"

"No, not at all," said Hamish, her attractions dimming a little like a faulty lightbulb. "See you there."

He climbed into the police Land Rover. Sonsie was in the passenger seat and Lugs in the back. "You're not creepy, are you?" he said. Sonsie gave a rumbling purr.

At the police station, he was met by local fisherman, Archie Maclean, carrying two mackerel. "Make you a nice wee dinner," he said, handing them over. "I saw you chasing after that flirty nurse."

"Why do you call her flirty?"

"Herself gets the Sundays off and aye gangs up tae the bar at the hotel and sits there till some fellow invites her for dinner."

"Surely not!"

"Aye. As sure as I'm standing here. If you're looking for Charlie, he's gone off with Priscilla."

"Why?" demanded Hamish.

"I dinnae ken. Take the fish."

"Thanks, Archie."

Hamish went slowly into the police station where he put the fish in the fridge. He was envious of Charlie's easy-going friendship with Priscilla. He wondered sourly whether Charlie was gay. He had shown no sexual interest in any female so far. But then one of his own best friends was Angela Brodie, the doctor's wife, and he could not ever remember lusting after her.

Curiosity overcame him. He told his animals to stay and went back out to his vehicle and sped off to the hotel.

The manager, Mr. Johnson, said they were down in the basement but he didn't know what they were doing. Hamish made his way down.

"This'll just be grand," he heard Charlie saying. "But maybe Hamish won't like it."

The voices were coming from the far end of the basement where a door stood open.

"Hamish won't like what?" he called.

There was a short silence and then Priscilla called, "In here."

Hamish walked in. He found himself in what seemed to have been a small apartment.

"What d'ye think?" cried Charlie. "Priscilla says I could move in here and you'd have more room at the station."

"What is this place?" asked Hamish.

"It used to be a wee apartment for the butler," said Charlie. The Tommel Castle Hotel had once been the Halburton-Smythes' private residence. When Colonel Halburton-Smythe had fallen on hard times, Hamish had persuaded him to turn the place into a hotel.

Hamish looked round. There was a small living room, furnished simply with a dusty gate-leg table and two hard chairs. By the side of the living room was a small kitchen with a tiny Belling cooker on a counter and some cups and plates covered with dust on the draining board beside a sink.

"The bedroom's through here," said Charlie eagerly. "Priscilla says that the butler, old Mr. Sweeney, was a great tall man."

The bedroom held a long single bed covered in an old mattress stuffed with ticking, flanked by two small chests of drawers.

"How do I square it wi' Strathbane?" asked Hamish.

"They don't need to know," said Priscilla.

Hamish suddenly realised that this could mean he would get his station back, all to himself. Perhaps he could even persuade one pretty nurse to join him there. He went off into a rosy dream.

Priscilla looked with some irritation at the tall sergeant with the flaming-red hair.

"Hamish! Wake up!"

"Oh, aye, grand," said Hamish quickly. "But make sure your phone works down here, Charlie. And God forbid we should have any more major crime, but if we do, you'll need to move back to the station."

"A home of my own!" cried Charlie, sitting down on one of the hard chairs which promptly splintered under his weight. He turned scarlet as he scrambled to his feet. "I'll repair that, Priscilla. I promise."

"Charlie, it was riddled with woodworm. There's plenty of furniture in the basement for you to choose from. I'll get a couple of the maids to help you."

"No," said Charlie firmly. "I'll do it all myself. I just need some cleaning stuff."

There were some cupboards under the sink. Priscilla bent down and looked into them.

"Well! Look at this? Our old butler seems to have nicked some of the best wines. And here's a bottle of vintage champagne. We'll have a glass each to celebrate."

"You mean the butler was a thief?" asked Charlie.

"It's called butler's privilege. He's dead anyway. I've found some glasses. I'll just rinse them out."

Hamish collected three sturdy chairs from an area of the basement outside, crowded with discarded furniture. Priscilla had just opened the bottle and was pouring out three glasses of champagne when Detective Jimmy Anderson walked into the apartment.

"What's this?" he demanded. "I was on my road to see you, Hamish, when I saw your Land Rover in the hotel car park. You know what I feel about drinking on duty. Got any whisky, Priscilla?"

Priscilla went to the cupboard and brought out a bottle of twelve-year-old malt.

"This do?"

Jimmy's blue eyes gleamed in his foxy face. "Pour it out, lassie."

"What brings you?" asked Hamish.

"Strathbane prison, that's what. I'm rounding up manpower. The search starts this afternoon. The number of weapons, drugs, and mobile phones has doubled in Scottish prisons."

"You could have phoned me," said Hamish.

"Och, I wanted a trip out. Blair is in charge and he's shouting and bullying already. We've got mobile phone detection equipment and drug dogs so the main search will be for weapons." Detective Chief Inspector Blair was the bane of Hamish Macbeth's life, always trying to get him transferred to Strathbane.

"You should be looking for bent screws," said Charlie. "If it's weapons, then the prison officers must be getting paid to sneak them in."

"Hard going," said Jimmy. "They all cover for each other."

His phone rang. He looked gloomily at the dial. "Blair," he said. "We'd best get going. Man, this whisky is heaven." He slipped the bottle in his pocket.

"You can stay," whispered Hamish to Charlie. "I'll

get Jimmy to say you couldnae leave the station un-
manned. But collect Sonsie and Lugs. I don't want
them left alone too long."

As they approached Strathbane, the skies darkened and
a smear of drizzle clouded Hamish's windscreen before
he switched the wipers on and looked down the long
road to where what he thought of as a boil on the Highlands appeared in the distance.

It had once been a thriving fishing port but the fishing stocks had declined and with it any heavy industry,
leaving the town a sink of crime and drugs. The prison
was a Victorian one, built to the same design as Worm-
wood Scrubs.

As they drove up to the entrance, the rain had become a torrent and the wind was rising, moaning in the
turrets of the old prison. After they had been through
security, a wooden-faced prison officer told them to report to the governor's office.

The governor, Bella Ogilvie, was a small, plump
woman. Beside her was a tall woman in police inspector's uniform. She had high Slavic cheekbones, cold
grey eyes, and a thin mouth.

"Where have you been, Anderson?" she snapped.

"Collecting reinforcements, ma'am," said Jimmy.
"You are…?"

"Fiona Herring. And no cracks about red herrings.
I've heard them all. Who's this?"

"Sergeant Hamish Macbeth, ma'am."

"Heard of you. The pair of you get over to C Wing and search all the cells."

"Where is Mr. Blair?" asked Jimmy.

"Mr. Blair is in hospital."

"What happened?"

Her eyes lit up and she suppressed a laugh. "The detective inspector insulted a police dog called Fred. He told the dog it was a mangy useless-looking cur and tried to kick it. Fred took offence and bit him in the arse. I have been called in from Inverness to take charge. Off with you."

As Hamish followed Jimmy to C Wing, he reflected that when she had nearly laughed, Fiona had suddenly appeared a very attractive woman.

At the end of a long dreary afternoon, they took their finds back to the governor's office: five knives, one replica gun, and a packet of Ecstasy tablets. The governor told them to take their contraband to the conference room.

Laid out on the long table was a depressing selection of drugs, phones, and weapons. The weapons consisted of knives, sharpened toothbrushes, shivs, and five guns.

"I have a list of the names and addresses of all the prison guards," said Inspector Fiona Herring. "I will allocate names to each officer. I want their backgrounds checked thoroughly. What is it, Governor?"

Mrs. Ogilvie looked like a frightened rabbit. "The guards have gone on strike," she wailed.

"Who is in charge of the union?"

"Blythe Cummings."

"I want him here. Now!"

The governor hurried off.

When it came Hamish's turn, Fiona said, "I think you may go back to your station, Sergeant. You have a large area to cover."

Lovely woman, thought Hamish. The first person in authority to realise the extent of my beat. No rings. Wonder if there's a man in her life.

When Hamish returned to his police station, he found Charlie loading up his old station wagon with his belongings. "You'd better come here every day and report for duty," said Hamish. "I'll miss your company in the evenings but not your big feet. You and Priscilla getting along all right?"

"She's great. Just like a sister."

Hamish pushed back his cap and scratched his red hair as he watched Charlie drive off. What man could survey the beauty that was Priscilla and look on her as a sister?

After Charlie had left, Hamish decided to drive to Braikie. His previous constable, Dick Fraser, had left to buy a bakery shop with a Polish woman called Anka. Anka was glamorous. Hamish had tried several times to get her out on a date but without success. Surely she and tubby Dick could not be romantically involved.

The shop had just closed for the night when he arrived. He noticed a shiny, brand-new BMW parked outside. If it was Dick's, business must be very good indeed.

He rang the bell to the flat over the shop. Anka Bajorak answered the door. My world is beginning to be peopled by beautiful unavailable women, thought Hamish. But maybe Gloria is available. Anka walked ahead of him up the stairs, her auburn hair tied back in a ponytail and her long legs encased in tight jeans, giving one highland police sergeant a stab of lust.

Dick had slimmed down. But with his grey hair and small figure, he certainly did not look like the type of man to capture the affections of such as Anka. He was comfortably ensconced in an armchair by the peat fire.

"It's yourself, Hamish," cried Dick. "Like a dram?"

"Tea will be fine."

"I'll get it," said Anka.

Hamish told Dick about the visit to the prison and then said, "There's a newcomer in the neighbourhood."

"That'll be the wee nurse," said Dick. "Talk o' the place. Say she dresses like a nurse out o' one o' thae *Carry On* movies. They say she's after the auld man's money."

"The things people say!" complained Hamish. "I've met her. She's charming."

"Oh aye? Got a date?"

"Next Sunday."

"Well, she wouldn't be going out wi' you if she was after money," said Dick.

Anka came back with a cup of tea for Hamish and two cakes. "How's business?" asked Hamish.

"Booming," said Anka. "We thought of opening another shop but we decided to start a business on the Internet. It's called BapsareUs. We send parcels of baps all over Britain."

"I'm not surprised," said Hamish. One of the usual Scottish laments was that it was almost impossible to get a decent bap, those large breakfast rolls. Anka's baps were famous.

"We've had to build a new place to cope with all the baking and take on lots of staff," said Anka. "Several of the big companies have tried to buy us over."

Hamish told them about Charlie moving out. "Won't you be lonely?" asked Dick.

"No, I'm delighted to get my station back. Charlie is great but he's so clumsy, he's a walking disaster."

"I would like to meet him," said Anka. "Bring him with you next time."

"Will do," said Hamish. "I'd better get back."

When Hamish returned to the station, he found a note on the kitchen table from Charlie. "I've taken Sonsie and Lugs up to the castle. They were mooching at the Italian restaurant and we don't want them getting fat. I'll drop them back later."

The wind had risen, moaning around the police station. Hamish fought off a sudden feeling of loneliness. But then he had a vision of the pretty Gloria, living with him at the police station. Three days to Sunday and then he would see her again.

Chapter Two

☠

Listen! You hear the grating roar
Of pebbles which the waves draw back, and fling,
At their return, up the high strand,
Begin, and cease, and then begin again,
With the tremulous cadence slow, and bring
The eternal note of sadness in.

—Matthew Arnold

Colonel Halburton-Smythe arrived back at the Tommel Castle Hotel in a bad mood. He and his wife had been visiting Lord and Lady Fortross over near Oban. Unfortunately, their room had been directly above the bedchamber of their hosts and the fireplace chimney acted as a splendid conduit of sound.

So on the first night, as he was getting ready for bed, he heard Lord Fortross's high complaining voice. "Why did you invite that boring little colonel? I can't abide retired military men who insist on keeping their titles. And the man's a damn stereotype."

The colonel had backed away from the fireplace as if before a snake and had told his startled wife to pack up. They were leaving in the morning.

He was an insecure little man, product of an ambitious father who had made his fortune with a chain of popular shoe shops. Using his fortune, his father had sent him to Eton and then on to Sandhurst Military Academy. The colonel had quickly adopted a personality to fit what he fondly believed was required. He worked hard and with his father's money, entertained lavishly. He rose rapidly up the ranks and married Philomena Halburton who hailed from an aristocratic family and had joined the name of Smythe to that of Halburton.

His happiest day was when he quit the army and bought the castle and estates, only to go nearly bankrupt after being tricked into bad investments. Hamish Macbeth saved the day with the hotel idea. Because of excellent fishing and shooting and a first-class manager, the hotel quickly prospered.

On his first day back, the colonel noticed a large man going down to the basement, someone he did not know. He went down and saw the man going into the old butler's apartment and followed him in. He blinked and looked around. A small coal fire was burning briskly. Two comfortable armchairs were drawn up beside it. A faded Chinese carpet that he remembered used to be in the morning room, now the hotel bar, covered the floor.

Standing by the fire was a giant of a man with fair hair and child-like blue eyes.

"Who the hell are you?" demanded the colonel.

So Charlie, in his soft lilting voice, explained while the colonel paced up and down.

"She had no right," raged the colonel. "Priscilla should have consulted me first."

"Well, sir," said Charlie. "Miss Priscilla did think it might be a good idea to have a resident polis, protecting the place. But I'll pack up. Maybe a wee dram, sir?"

The colonel suddenly sighed and sat down in one of the armchairs, all bluster gone. The cosy little room reminded him of the days of his childhood, before his father had become so rich and ambitious. They had lived in a neat little bungalow, warm and safe.

"Yes, I will have a dram," he said.

Charlie poured two stiff drinks and then sat down opposite.

"Tell me about yourself," he said. So Charlie talked about his upbringing in South Uist in the Hebrides, his soft voice lulling the colonel into a rare feeling of peace.

The colonel was suddenly overcome with a desire to tell this gentle giant about his humiliation. Charlie listened carefully. When the colonel had finished, Charlie said, "I mind Lord Fortross. I was visiting relatives in Tiree and himself was over for the snipe shooting. Awful pompous git. Nobody liked him. Talk about bores! Man, he was describing himself."

The colonel beamed and stretched his feet out to the fire. "Any more whisky, laddie?"

Hamish heard a knock at the door later that day and found Priscilla on the doorstep. "I came to say good-bye," she said. "I'm off to London tomorrow. Dad has discovered Charlie."

"Oh, my," said Hamish. "Is he out on his ear?"

"It's the oddest thing. He's taken Charlie trout fishing."

"It isnae the season."

"Sea trout. The pair of them are out on the loch."

"Well, I'm blessed. Aren't you surprised?"

"Not really. Charlie is so kind. All sorts of people gravitate to him."

Hamish's hazel eyes narrowed with jealousy. Did Priscilla fancy him? Then he relaxed. If she was interested in Charlie, she would not be leaving for London.

When they had been engaged, she had been so passionless. Had that been his fault?

"You've gone off into a dream, Hamish," said Priscilla.

"Sorry. I was just thinking how nice and quiet it is now."

"Are Dick and Anka an item?"

"No. Business partners. No romance there."

"I wouldn't be too sure."

"C'mon, Priscilla. Don't be daft. Tubby wee grey-haired Dick and the glorious Anka!"

That evening in the bakery, Anka went upstairs to the living room and found Dick dressed in his best suit. "Are you going out somewhere?" she asked. "That's the suit you wear when we've a meeting with the bank manager. And roses and champagne! What's the occasion? Dick, you've gone quite white."

Dick sank to one knee and held up a small jeweller's box. "Will you do me the very great honour of marrying me?" he said.

Anka threw back her head and laughed. Red in the face, Dick got to his feet. "I'm sorry," he said. "I should have known there wasnae any hope."

"Give me the ring, open the champagne, my love. I thought you would never ask."

Charlie went about his duties during the day, visiting the outlying croft houses to make sure everything was all right. In the evenings, he was now expected to take his dinner with the colonel and his wife and then they all retreated to his little flat for a nightcap. Mrs. Halburton-Smythe was delighted with her husband's new friendship. She had never before known him to be so relaxed and so amiable.

She would have liked to invite Hamish to join them but the colonel stubbornly refused to have anything to do with that "lazy, mooching copper." He had snobbery enough to hope that his beautiful daughter might make a good match and he always feared she might have the folly to become engaged to Hamish again.

On Sunday, Hamish brushed his red hair until it shone, put on his best suit, and made his way to the restaurant. He had reserved a table by the window. The evening was still and the first frost had arrived. The waiter, Willie Lamont, who was once his constable before he married the restaurant owner's daughter, approached with the menu.

"Two menus," said Hamish. "I'm expecting company."

"And who would that be?"

"Mind your own business."

Willie went off and came back with another menu. "What's special tonight?" asked Hamish.

"Something sounds like awfy bokey."

"Probably osso buco," said Hamish, who was used to Willie's malapropisms.

Hamish waited and waited. At last, he found Mr. Harrison's number and phoned. An Eastern European voice answered—the Latvian, Hamish guessed.

"May I speak to Miss Dainty?" he asked. "This is

Hamish Macbeth. She was supposed to meet me for dinner this evening."

"Mr. Harrison said she went for a walk. Hasn't come back."

Probably forgot, thought Hamish dismally, after he had rung off. He ordered the osso buco but picked at it, finally gave up, paid the bill, and went back to the station.

"For the first time in my life," he said to his animals, "I could do wi' a nice wee crime to take my mind off things."

Two days went by while Hamish stubbornly stopped himself from phoning the hunting lodge to find out why Gloria had stood him up. It was a fine autumn day. The rowan trees planted at some of the cottage gates to keep the fairies away were bowed down with scarlet berries. The lower slopes of the two tall mountains behind the village were purple with heather.

He took a stroll along the waterfront. He saw the Currie sisters, Nessie and Jessie, approaching and looked wildly round for some means of escape, but they had seen him, so he waited reluctantly until they came up to him. They were unmarried twins and looked remarkably alike with tightly permed grey hair, thick glasses, and identical camel-hair coats.

"I'm glad to see Mr. Harrison's got himself a proper nurse," said Nessie, "and not some wee flibbertigibbet."

"Flibbertigibbet," echoed the Greek chorus that was her sister.

"You mean Gloria Dainty has left?" exclaimed Hamish.

"Went off wi' her suitcase," said Nessie. "Never even left a note."

"When was this?"

"Sunday evening."

Hamish felt a sharp pang of unease. He touched his cap to them and moved on. Suddenly he decided to go out to the hunting lodge.

Juris, the Latvian, answered the door. He was a tall, powerful man. Hamish asked to see Mr. Harrison but was told the old man was lying down and did not want to be disturbed.

"Why did Miss Dainty leave?" asked Hamish. "You were supposed to run her to Lochdubh to have dinner with me on Sunday evening."

"I went to fetch her but she was not there and all her belongings had gone," said Juris. "On Monday, Mr. Harrison got a new nurse up from an agency in Inverness."

"Didn't she leave a note?"

"No, nothing."

"But when I phoned, you said she'd gone for a walk."

"That's what Mr. Harrison told me. The next day, my wife looked in her room and saw all her things were gone and told him, and he said, 'Good riddance.'"

"Was Miss Dainty involved with a man?"

"If she was, she didn't talk about it."

Hamish could not get any further. He went back to the police station and rang around all the local taxi companies, but Gloria had not called for a taxi. So it followed that someone must have been waiting for her at the end of the drive.

Well, she had gone, and that was that.

A day later, a burglary was reported at an ironmonger's in Braikie. Hamish called Charlie, picked him up at the hotel, and sped off. The owner, a tall highlander called Josh Andrews, pointed to the door. "It looks as if they opened it with a crowbar," he said.

"What was taken?" asked Hamish.

"I have a list right here."

Hamish looked down a long list of expensive power tools. "I'd better get the forensic boys over," he said. "We'll need to look for fingerprints. Have you contacted the insurance company?"

"Not yet."

"They'll want to send an investigator."

"What for?" demanded Josh angrily. "You see the door's been jemmied. You've got the list. Chust put in your report, laddie."

"It is like this," said Hamish gently. "Shopkeepers often stage a burglary when they fall on hard times. And their investigators are like ferrets. They'll search and search to make sure you're not pulling a fast one.

I 'member some poor soul ower in Cnothan. Faked a burglary and got a criminal record."

"Are you calling me a liar?"

"Waud I dae a cruel thing like that," said Hamish, his accent strengthening. "I'll chust be having a wee keek out back."

"What for?"

"They could have escaped that way. I gather it took place at night?"

"Must have done."

"So they would not want to be seen loading stuff out on the main street. Stand aside."

"No, you need a warrant."

"Don't be daft," said Charlie. He moved forward and picked up the large man as if he weighed nothing at all and set him to one side.

"*No!*" shouted Josh, and a tear rolled down one cheek.

Hamish looked at Charlie. "Do you see any signs of a break-in?"

"Cannae say I do, sir."

Hamish handed Josh back his list. "Listen to me. I cannot be bothered charging you. I know times are hard. Put a big sign in your window saying 'Autumn Sale. Everything Must Go. Everything Reduced.' Then you knock a couple of quid off the items you said were stolen along with everything else. Folk love to think they're getting a bargain."

"I'm sorry," said Josh brokenly.

"Oh, get off your sorry arse and get to work," said Hamish. "Come along, Charlie."

"It's a shame," said Charlie as they climbed into the Land Rover.

"Never mind," said Hamish. "There's a grand wee café up the coast on the road to Kinlochbervie. We'll have a cup of coffee and a bun. It's a grand day."

The café was called Westering Home. There were two tables outside facing a long curve of white sandy beach. Hamish and Charlie contentedly drank coffee and munched currant buns until Hamish reluctantly said they had better be getting back.

They were driving along the one-track road beside the beach where two boys were playing when Hamish suddenly flung on the brakes and screeched to a halt. Lugs, in the back, let out a startled yelp.

"What's up?" asked Charlie.

But Hamish was out and running towards the boys.

"Where did you get that?" he demanded.

A small tousle-haired child held up a dripping wet nurse's cap. "It just floated in," he said. "We wasnae doing anything wrong."

Charlie had followed Hamish. "What's up?"

"Unless I am mistaken, that's thon missing nurse's cap," said Hamish, taking a forensic bag out of his pocket and sliding the cap in. "Let's search around a bit before we call Strathbane."

"Strong currents here, I've heard," said Charlie. "If she's in the sea, she could be halfway to America. Here, you boys. Names and addresses and I'll call on your parents later."

When the boys had scampered off, Hamish said, "I'll take the west end of the beach and you try the east."

Hamish made his way to where the cliffs rose up against the pale-blue sky. Seagulls wheeled and dived. All the while, his mind worked busily. She surely wouldn't have left wearing her nurse's uniform. At the foot of the cliffs were jagged needle rocks like pointing fingers. As he approached, two things struck him. That old familiar smell of death and the buzzing of flies.

With a beating heart, he picked his way among the rocks. Between two of the pointing rocks lay the shattered body of Gloria Dainty under a heaving canopy of blackflies.

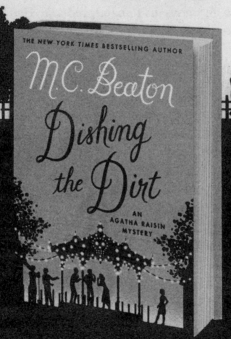

VISIT US ONLINE AT

WWW.HACHETTEBOOKGROUP.COM

FEATURES:

**OPENBOOK BROWSE AND
SEARCH EXCERPTS**

•

AUDIOBOOK EXCERPTS AND PODCASTS

•

AUTHOR ARTICLES AND INTERVIEWS

•

**BESTSELLER AND PUBLISHING
GROUP NEWS**

•

SIGN UP FOR E-NEWSLETTERS

•

**AUTHOR APPEARANCES AND TOUR
INFORMATION**

•

SOCIAL MEDIA FEEDS AND WIDGETS

•

DOWNLOAD FREE APPS

BOOKMARK HACHETTE BOOK GROUP
@ WWW.HACHETTEBOOKGROUP.COM